The Miracle of Christmas

Morris Fenris

The Miracle of Christmas

TABLE OF CONTENTS

CHAPTER 1

As she arrived at the apartment she shared with her husband Robert, Emma Larsson found his car missing.

Thank goodness!

She took the stairs to their unit, pleased she was just in time to start dinner before he returned from work.

“Hi Emma!“ Ingrid, her neighbor on the first floor, called as she walked past. “Thanks for the pecan pie last night. Ida and I enjoyed it tremendously.“

She turned to smile at the sweet old lady who had been a delight since she'd moved in with Robert after the wedding.

“My pleasure Ingrid, I'm glad you enjoyed it.“

“Don't listen to her, Em. I had barely a bite before she wolfed it down. Her belly is greedy,“ Ida, Ingrid's sister, hollered from inside the apartment.

“Shush Ida! You wouldn't blame me for your cataract acting up and stopping you from sticking the fork right.” Ingrid retorted. “I don't have a greedy belly!“

Emma bit back a chuckle as Ingrid hushed her and led her farther away from the door.

“Would you mind writing out the recipe for me? I would really like to surprise my friends on bridge night,“ she whispered, her eyes shining with hopefulness as she darted a glance behind to see if Ida was standing there.

“Of course, it's an old recipe that has been passed down my family for generations. I’ll write it and bring it down later.“

“Thanks, dear, you are a blessing.“ Ingrid replied with a

warm smile and patted her hands. “Let me return before that snoop Ida comes to stick her nose in what is none of her business.“

Emma bent to kiss her cheeks and flashed her a conspiratorial grin as she took the remaining stairs to her flat.

Ingrid Myers was a disaster in the kitchen, if you took the time to listen to Ida, her long-suffering sister.

The only form of cooking she could manage was to warm soups from cans and brew coffee. But, bless her soul, she never gave up trying to cook and sailed from one kitchen failure to the next. Despite setting the smoke alarm off countless times, she never relented in her efforts. Emma loved the stubborn old lady immensely.

Closing the door with a quiet click, Emma stood just inside their two bedroom flat currently called home to inhale the beautiful scent of jasmine and honeysuckle. She was a sucker for fresh flowers and couldn't wait till they saved enough to get their own small, quaint house in the suburbs.

Emma closed her eyes and imagined a vivid periwinkle blue and linen white with floral designs painted along the edges. Shaded by a tree or two with a little flower garden in front, the lawn would always stay immaculately trimmed

Shaking herself from the pleasant daydream, Emma removed her shoes and went into the bathroom for a quick shower while she thought of what to make for dinner.

She always loved to surprise Robert with a new meal every evening and was delighted when his eyes lit up over the delicious-looking food. His dramatic expressions filled her with satisfaction and watching him eat was such a pleasure.

Experimenting and planning meals was one of her numerous hobbies, and she constantly battled with restraint. More often than not, she ended up making a little too much food. Enough leftovers remained to feed an extra two. Emma was glad for Ingrid and Ida living just below because she cringed to think she'd have to waste good food.

Robert constantly teased her about quitting her job at the newspaper agency in Magnificent Miles. They could live high and mighty if she opened a restaurant in the middle of the city to make them some money. She usually laughed it off, taking a swipe at him. Deep within, though, she nursed the idea.

From the first time her mother had tied an apron around her seven-year-old waist and placed her on a kitchen stool, this passion for cooking had been born.

She'd taken some cooking classes during summer in high school and knew how to cook more than the basics.

Being in the kitchen gave Emma a thrill that was almost akin to an adrenaline rush, and she was beyond thrilled Robert had a big appetite.

On a few occasions, he'd stroll into the kitchen and stay out of the way while he watched her with undisguised fascination. He once commented while they cuddled on the couch after a quiet dinner that he'd never seen anyone who enjoyed cooking as much as she did, including his mother who'd won countless county fair blue ribbons for her famous lasagna.

Emma beamed as she dried off from the shower and padded barefoot across the room to put on a robe.

Thoughts of Robert always left her feeling like a young teenager with a huge, lopsided grin on her face and butterflies fluttering around in her stomach.

They were technically newlyweds, having just tied the knot in a small, close-knit spring wedding in early May, barely seven months ago. Being married to Robert felt like walking on clouds in a state of never-ending euphoric bliss. Especially when she'd wake up in the middle of the night to stare with overwhelming emotions at his relaxed sleeping face.

She was the luckiest women in the entire world to have Robert love her so deeply. They'd met on a pleasant March afternoon at Northwestern University, Evanston. From the first stolen looks they exchanged, they had known they were meant to be together. Emma told anyone who cared to listen. Right from the moment she'd observed him tutoring in the cafeteria.

She'd been initially struck by his patience and calmness while tutoring the young girl, a popular trust-fund freshman, who had not paid any attention to the topic he'd spent almost thirty minutes carefully explaining to her. When he had caught Emma staring at him, she'd smiled encouragingly and continued sipping her coffee.

Soon after, the girl who was wearing too much makeup for the extremely hot afternoon and loudly smacking her chewing gum, stood up and declared she was going to hang out with friends. She hadn't understood a word of what he'd been explaining and didn't think she needed the mechanical parts of an airplane when she was done with college. She had declared that a job in her father's company was already waiting for her.

As the girl sashayed out, he had sighed and gathered his notes, the half empty cup of coffee, and had walked over to join Emma.

“Hi, I’m Robert. I wasn't that bad, was I?“ he had asked, extending his hand to her.

She'd laughed, color suffusing her cheeks, as she took his firm warm hand. “No you weren't. I don't think she likes airplanes.“

His laughter, unrestrained and straight from the belly, had thrown Emma into a state of giggles. They had spent the next thirty seconds trying and failing to control their fits of hilarity enough to have a normal conversation. From that moment, they'd been inseparable.

Thinking back, she remembered Robert as tall and built like a football player. It was a wonder he couldn't play the sports. He had mischievous twinkling eyes that contrasted with his body size and gave him an easy-going appearance which usually put people at ease around him.

Emma always felt like a delicate waif whenever she stood close to him. It secretly made her feel wondrously good. Kind and compassionate, he had dropped out of college before graduation to work two jobs when his mother was diagnosed with the late stages of ovarian cancer.

When she died a month later, his father, unable to cope with the reality of life without his wife, suffered a massive stroke almost immediately and died. Robert had buried both his parents in the space of three months.

Blinking back tears, Emma now stood in the kitchen remembering the mild depression and how he'd withdrawn from everything following their deaths. It took time, patience and a lot of love for Emma to draw him out of the shell he'd barricaded himself within during those dark times.

As they persevered and managed to stay above the waters during those black days, Joy eventually returned. Now they were happily married and on their way to celebrating their one-year anniversary. Emma couldn't be any more thankful as she sent a silent prayer heavenward.

***

Robert Larsson smiled, watching his wife sway gently as she peeled potatoes while Kirk Franklin's *Alleluia* played from the portable music player atop the refrigerator. Her fingers moved deftly like a still-life artist with a paintbrush as she sliced and diced precisely, her concentration unwavering even as she moved accordingly to the beat of the music.

He never got tired of watching her.

When she walked, when she ate, when she slept and danced; he loved to watch her and hear her light and airy laughter. She was like a cold breeze on a hot day. It soothed him every time, even when he was swarmed with so many racing thoughts about the future. He just had to look at Emma's beautiful smile, and everything would feel easier and a whole lot better.

She was sunshine on a dark stormy day. Everything she did and touched, she added a drop of goodness. When he was going through a dark period, she'd come into his life. He had been overwhelmed by one tragedy after another with destructive thoughts pushing him toward the edge. Her unwavering strength and encouragement had kept him from toppling over and drowning in a desolate river of loss and depression.

Without her, he knew things could have only gotten worse.

Robert cleared his throat after a while of admiring his wife and chuckled when she jumped and whirled, her eyes flashing in mock annoyance.

"That wasn't funny, Mr. Larsson. You'll give me a coronary one day, I tell you!"

He grabbed her by the middle and kissed her soft lips. "Only if it would keep you with me forever, then I wouldn't mind at all."

She hit him playfully on the shoulder. "Go on, you! You just delight in spoiling my fun."

Robert wiggled his eyebrows like a desperado. "Mission

accomplished. The good Lord would be so proud of me. It's a grave sin to be having any fun without your husband, you should know better than that, Mrs. Larsson.“

Emma doubled over in laughter. “And where did you get that from, Mr. Larsson? I've never come across that particular commandment before.“

“Yeah well, you know how. So adhere,“ Robert replied, wagging a finger at her.

Emma held him close and rolled her eyes dramatically. “Yeah well, you have no issues in that department. Having fun alone grows boring eventually.“

“Thank heavens, then!“ He replied with a smile and watched as a dark shadow fell over her face and her mood changed a little.

“Why are you quiet, my lovely woman? Your lips are pursed in that manner I know so well. Come on. Spill,“ Robert urged as he gazed gently into her beautiful brown eyes, the shade of caramel.

Emma couldn't hide her feelings to save her life.

Blessed with an expressive face, her emotions were always open, and he was familiar with every single one of them.

“Tell me we will remain this overwhelmingly happy, darling. I never want to stop feeling this way,” she whispered and tightened her arms around him.

Robert smiled and tucked a lock of brown curl behind her ear, emotions clogging his throat.

He felt the same way and, despite all the ruckus going on at work now, he never had time for unhappiness because Emma was waiting at home.

“I promise to keep you safe and continuously happy, that

these thoughts would never find a resting place in your heart."

Emma beamed like flowers opening to accept the light of the sun. "Thanks, baby."

Robert kissed her nose and spoiled the emotional euphoric moment by wagging his eyebrow in his trademark fashion.

Emma laughed and shoved him away as she turned back to the vegetables on the kitchen table.

"What is for dinner, Martha Stewart?" Robert teased as he perused the contents on the counter.

Emma always had something up her sleeves. He reckoned, before the end of the year, he would have to sign up for a gym membership.

She turned with a grin and a sly tilt to her eyes. "It's a surprise involving sirloin and stock."

Lifting the back of his hand to his forehead, Robert rolled his eyes to simulate his delight. He planted a loud smacking kiss on her cheeks. "Do your magic, woman!"

"Shoo! Out with you. I can't concentrate with all your distracting kisses," she said, pushing him gently out of the kitchen.

"I'm leaving already. Easy..."

With his hands held high, he exited the kitchen to the living room where his favorite baseball game reruns were airing.

He settled comfortably on the couch and adjusted the TV's volume while the aroma of whatever magic Emma was concocting drifted through the open doorway.

A few minutes into the game, Robert's thoughts returned to the dilemma he'd found himself strapped in at work. His brows furrowed as pressure from the unknown rested heavily on his shoulders, and his thoughts raced like horses at the Derby.

Almost an hour later, Emma's jolt pulled his confused tired mind out of the deep dive. He planted on a false smile and followed her to the dining table. The disturbing thoughts were shelved further in the recesses of his head, as he prepared to eat the delight laid out on the table.

CHAPTER 2

Emma felt a deep sense of foreboding as she stepped into the foyer of The Miles Press the next morning. Everyone skittered around with a bubbling sense of expectancy.

"Good morning, Rebecca, how are you?" She spoke to the ginger-haired receptionist who replaced the receiver on the telephone and assembled the scattered papers across her desk before looking up at her.

"Morning, Emma, you are just in time."

"Just in time for what?" She asked as she watched Trevor Gates, the publicist for the agency, exit his cubicle and head for the Management office.

"You need to call Caroline," the receptionist told her.

Caroline Meyers, her controversy-loving colleague at the press, always had her ear open for work gossip. Emma called to find out that she'd overhead Larry Bishop on the phone saying that big changes would occur in the press in the coming days, and everyone should gear up for the worst.

"You know better than to be eavesdropping behind closed doors, Caroline," Emma reproached her.

"If I did stop, how would any of you keep abreast with office issues that would eventually come to bite you in the gut?" Caroline replied, her voice smug and uncaring.

Emma laughed and quizzed her thoroughly about everything else she heard. Caroline's response was a sharp "tsk" before she proceeded to spill Larry's discussion.

As it turned out, she didn't know much about what was really going on, but it seemed like someone in the managerial board would be leaving soon.

Emma thanked her for the tidbit of information and hung up. Then sat for the next thirty minutes mulling quietly over the conversation. Immediately after graduating from college, Emma had gotten a job at The Miles Press, a local newspaper agency in Magnificent Miles, downtown Chicago.

She had secured the badly needed job to help Robert pay off medical loans at the Francine Rivers Hospital in Evanston where his mother had been admitted during her illness.

This was after he'd reapplied back to college in the fall. Balancing two jobs and night classes had taken a huge toll on him. Her heart broke every time she saw the telltale stress lines on his face.

Emma had been lucky to run into an old friend of her father's at the coffee shop on Main Street. She usually hung out with a group of friends—Jessica, Susie Ann, Lynn, and Delores—who were also fellow book club members at the same coffee shop.

After exchanging pleasantries, the old friend asked if her job search had yielded anything positive. A recent lunch with her father had informed him of her graduation from Northwestern with a degree in journalism and press relations.

Shaking her head regrettably, she almost went catatonic in excitement when he told her of a discrete opening at Magnificent Miles Local Newspaper Agency which was better known as The Miles Press. It was located just thirty-two minutes away from Evanston through the subway station. Emma had been searching for a job for almost three months and hadn't much luck finding one. She was beyond herself with happiness.

When she'd told Robert of the fabulous news, he'd been as

thrilled as she was. He'd taken the time to ring her very early the next morning, so she could get up in time to prepare for the interview scheduled for nine o'clock. He knew how forgetful she was with setting alarm clocks. Whenever she managed to remember, she always placed the alarm as far from her bedside table as possible.

Dressed in a smart-looking pencil skirt and a simple cream-colored silk shirt, Emma had taken the train to Magnificent Miles for the interview with a nervous half frown on her face.

The interview had gone remarkably well as the interviewer had tried to make her as comfortable as possible with reassuring smiles and witty anecdotes. After thirty minutes, she was hired immediately and asked to resume the next Monday.

Emma left the Press with a spring to her step and raced back home to share the news with Robert. She'd since worked at the Press for three years and a few months. Aside from the poor salary she earned and the heavy workload sometimes, the agency had gone on to become something of an extended family.

Emma got along well with everyone including her boss; Dahlia Pritchard.

Often times, Dahlia treated her like a daughter more than an employee and was always there with a nod of approval for each milestone crossed.

"There is an emergency meeting in the next thirty minutes, and it seems like something is about to go down." Rebecca whispered to Emma, as she stood up to submit some documents in the nearest cubicle to her.

Emma hoped it wasn't a progression outreach report. Those usually were tense and uncomfortable, especially when it dropped significantly. She walked to her cubicle, placed her bag on her desk and looked around covertly for Caroline.

It wasn't that big of a deal, but she wanted to avoid Caroline catching her in the wrong place and acting like it was all a top-secret, information-ring bust.

She almost jumped out of her skin when Caroline whisper loudly above her shoulder, "Who do you think it'll be?"

"Caroline. Come on, you are a grown woman. Stop sneaking up on people," Emma chided as she turned her chair towards her unrepentant colleague. Unfazed, she rested her hip on the edge of her desk and grinned at her.

"So, you haven't speculated on who is leaving or anything about the meeting?"

Emma shrugged and stretched a little. "I'm interested, but I think it's probably a progress report. You're thinking negative thoughts, aren't you, Carol?"

Caroline rolled her eyes. "Yeah well, I'm usually right nine out of ten."

The beep, signaling a meeting, stopped Emma from replying. Caroline walked to her cubicle to pick up a pad and pen. Everyone on the floor headed towards the conference room where meetings of the sorts were usually held while whispering amongst themselves.

Emma hoped everything was alright. She caught up with Caroline who had a pleased look on her face like she knew something no one else did.

***

Robert bit back a retort as he glared at the Southwest Airlines ramp supervisor who was Robert's immediate boss, Richard Bloomfield. He sat across from him Richard as the man studied him.

The ramp supervisor, dressed in a charcoal black suit and pristine white shirt, twirled an expensive-looking gold pen in his hand. With every turn, the bright white light above struck the brilliant sleek gold Rolex on his left wrist.

Richard was someone who got what he wanted one way or the other. He played on both sides of the fence; always having his cake with extra icing and all the trimmings alongside.

Robert disliked that greatly but was always polite and civil to the man. But sitting in front of him now, his thoughts were far from polite or even civil. Two months ago, Robert had happened over a huge discrepancy while he was loading some baggage into the baggage compartment.

Robert couldn't stop the suitcase he was transferring into the ULD from crashing to the ground. Out of the damaged suitcase spilled satchels of white powdery substances that left him rooted to the spot for a couple of seconds. Before the baggage got to the ramp, they were thoroughly searched by the airport security agents. Robert wondered how the suitcase had managed to evade the security search and proceeded to the ramp. He snapped out of his shocked state quickly and reported the suitcase to Richard who expressed a similar surprise at the whole incident. He dismissed Robert back to the ramp and made a call to the airport agents who confiscated the suitcase and its content.

After the incident, Robert became more particular about the baggage he loaded into the planes and reported any suspicious findings to his boss. Robert was signing off at work the next Friday when he saw an unknown man wearing a black hoodie and a low-slung cap hand over a parcel to Richard who tucked it inside his coat and made for his office.

More out of curiosity than suspicion, Robert followed discreetly and overhead Richard confirm the delivery of the package to someone on the phone and speak about expectations of a wire to his accounts in the next minute. He had then promised the last mishap wouldn't happen again and the loose end would be handled.

When Robert tried to leave the spot, he hid behind after the startling discovery, Richard turned at that moment. The two men stood staring at each other for a few uncomfortable seconds before Richard invited him into his office.

By body size and features, they were both different as night and day. While Robert was huge and stockier, Richard was on the slender side with long bony limbs.

Robert shoved away the negative images swirling in his head but watched Robert with wary and sharp keen eyes. Richard had no scruples and would not hesitate to cover his tracks in the most nefarious ways possible.

Richard placed the cards on the table and admitted the underhanded activities in which he was involved. He quietly threatened Robert that it would be in his best interest to keep mute about it and leave the status quo alone.

Robert spoke angrily for the first time to his boss of over four years. He wouldn't be part of an illegal practice and would only do the right thing in that situation. Richard had only smiled and told him the consequences of his actions would be the loss of his job and the manipulation of the entire operation so that blame and guilt would fall directly on his lap.

He was a supervisor and Robert an ordinary ramp agent. It only took stuffing a suitcase with drugs and reporting to the security agents that he'd caught Robert in the act.

He would be publicly humiliated and worse, end up in jail.

Robert had been given two weeks to decide. Either he spilled the beans to the director or kept mute and continued to receive a percentage of the cut from each run. Robert watched Richard, wearing a mocking smile, wait patiently for his decision. Richard spoke up finally after a minute.

"You know this would benefit you, Robert. Since salaries have been slashed for almost a year now, I know you need every dollar you can get. You can buy a house. I heard you talking to a friend some weeks ago about wanting to surprise your wife with a new house before Christmas."

"I don't want to buy a house for my wife with that kind of money!" Robert answered, as he silently vowed not to fall into this web of deceit and crime.

"Nonsense," Richard said dismissively. "Everyone is trying hard to get enough money to settle outstanding bills and this is not as strange as what some other people have done. Stop acting like a saint and think."

Robert shook his head in frustration and stood up to leave. "I can't do this. I can't live with my conscience. This is totally wrong."

Richard stood, too, with a dangerous look in his eyes. "Then you have to keep that mouth of yours shut or face going down for this, because I can turn this whole deal around and make you the bad guy. Think of what the outcome of that would be. You would be arrested and sent to jail."

Robert stiffened and stood still for a moment before walking out of the office and slamming the door with pent up frustration.

Walking into the airline's lunchroom, he sat down heavily and stared at the delicious sandwich Emma had made for him that morning. It didn't look so good anymore as his thoughts raced and a cloud of despair settled over him.

He couldn't afford to lose this job. Unpaid bills abounded and he was trying his best to pay them off before Christmas. He really wanted to celebrate the New Year with Emma in their new home. It was supposed to be the best Christmas surprise ever.

Now, Robert was sinking deep into something that could end disastrously, and he was beyond confused. He didn't want to worry Emma with any of this and hoped he'd find an answer fast to make this all go away and still do the right thing in the process.

Robert did the only thing he could manage at that moment. He closed his eyes and prayed.

CHAPTER 3

When everyone was settled in the conference room and the secretary stood ready to take notes, Dahlia Pritchard, the head manager of The Miles Press, stood with a sad smile and announced her resignation from the Agency.

A chorus of loud gasps travelled around the room. Melanie Cartwright, a gossip columnist and resident mother hen, released a loud dramatic groan. Emma sighed as Dahlia thanked everyone for a pleasant working environment and gave her reasons for resigning.

She and her husband, Mark, had been married for almost twenty-five years now. They'd promised each other to retire in their fifties and spend the next years travelling around the world and sending post cards to their children and grandchildren. Mark, who'd retired for close to two years now, had been waiting for her to celebrate her 50th birthday, so she could retire too, and they could begin the next adventurous stage of their lives.

Almost everyone sighed and a few approving sounds were made over the sweet plans the couple had made. Congratulations were offered to Dahlia, some lamenting on how much they'd miss her.

Mike Grayson, an editor at the press, asked about the new manager and Dahlia told the expectant faces around the room that the new manager had been appointed already and would resume in a few days or earlier.

Emma sent her a woebegone look as their soon-to-be retired manager sat down. She smiled when the older woman blew her a kiss. Everyone loved Dahlia because she was such a kind and warm human being and a patient, encouraging boss.

A tug on the hem of her blouse took her attention away from

the faces of the press employees. Emma turned to Caroline who had been the one needing her attention.

"Why do you have the expression of the cat who ate the canary? Everyone will be bawling the first chance they get, but you have a satisfied smile."

Caroline bent to whisper in her ears as Dahlia's secretary stood up to announce the columnist of the week. "I'm glad she's resigned. I never did like her too much."

Emma's eyes widened in surprise at Caroline who continued in defense of her words. "She is terribly biased and plays a lot of favoritism. Besides, she never liked me. Why should I hang my head over about her departure?"

"Caroline, you can be quite difficult sometimes. Admit it. You do certain things that aren't exactly nice," Emma replied with disapproval.

Caroline's eyes flashed with quick anger before a fake smile replaced it. "Well, she is gone now, ain't she? She never did understand good journalism."

Emma shook her head. Caroline Meyers could be quite a handful. In the past, she was rumored to discredit other journalists to take over particular assignments through deceptive means. Although most people avoided her, Caroline liked her dry humor and had witnessed her rare acts of kindness. She was also, undoubtedly, one of the best journalists at the press.

It was true Dahlia came down hard on her a lot, but she was justified in her actions. Caroline could get out of hand quite easily if she was left unguided.

Emma straightened just in time to hear her name being called for the columnist of the week award and her mouth fell open.

She stood, a blush creeping up her cheeks as everyone cheered, and went forward to receive the funny looking award. It was shaped like a screaming mouth, something the agency usually gave out to the columnist with the best interactions for the previous week.

She heard a catcall from the back and saw Shelly, the mischievous assistant to the PR, wink at her.

"Congratulations, Emma! You'll only do better," Dahlia said to her from where she sat.

"Hear, hear!" Gary, the editor from first floor, cheered and everyone clapped loudly.

Emma grew suddenly shy, twirling the award nervously, as she stood facing her fellow employees. This was the fourth time the award was passed to her and every time she held it and had to give a mandatory speech, she was always left tongue-tied and nervous.

There were more fabulous writers at the press.

Gary Saltzman who wrote entertainment daily. Wendy Cole who covered travel and holiday destinations along with a score of others. She was continuously surprised that her *Fix It by Emma* corner column garnered a lot of publicity and was fast becoming a main column in the press daily paper.

She cleared her throat noisily and blushed harder when Gary crooned about how beautiful her face looked flushed, and Shelly yelled, "Shut it, Cowboy! She is happily married, and her husband is big enough to take you apart."

Everybody laughed uproariously, as Gary threw them a dirty look and begged her to run away with him.

"I'm sorry, Gary. I don't think a certain gentleman would be too pleased about that," She said to Gary who placed a hand over his heart and let his mouth hang open in playful shock.

“I want to thank everyone for this…again,” Emma continued as she swept the entire room with her eyes, a sincere smile on her face. She turned to regard Dahlia with warmth. “But I think this moment should be about Dahlia. Thank you for being such an amazing boss and putting up with all of our excesses.”

Almost everyone in the room agreed good-naturedly and some blew a kiss at the beaming woman.

“I have a suggestion to make, though. I propose we have a little going-away party in honor of her this evening. Nothing overly fancy. Just pizza and wine after work is done.”

“Why that's a fabulous idea, Emma! You always come up with the sweetest things,” Wendy Cole said.

“Oh yeah, you always do,” Caroline echoed, her tone slightly sarcastic as she glanced away.

Emma ignored her and filled everyone in on the plans for the party she’d formulated in her head a few minutes after Dahlia had made her announcement.

There was so much to be done and calls to be made. She also had to put the finishing touches on her column for the morning paper and reply some *Fix It by Emma* emails that'd been sent in that morning.

She couldn't wait to tell Robert all about the award and Dahlia's going away party, so she escaped to the bathroom immediately after the meeting was over to call him.

After three tries, he still wasn't picking up. Emma went back to work and waited for him to return the call.

After work, Emma dragged her exhausted body up the stairs and met Ida, Ingrid's sister, on the way. Ida, a complete opposite of her plump sister, was slender as a reed with her gray hair pulled back in a severe bun. Poised on her straight thin nose were tortoiseshell glasses from which she peered at Emma with a sour expression.

Also, in heavy contrast to her sister's naturally warm and friendly disposition, Ida always wore a displeased, disapproving purse to her lips.

"Why has Ingrid been walking around with a gleam in her eyes like she is up to something?" She demanded. "I hope you aren't encouraging her about continuing her foolhardy escapades with the horrible thoughts that she can cook. I would stand no longer to be woken up at night with the smell of burnt food or served dinner, which she swears are take outs, and have the taste of something despicable on my tongue all night."

"Oh, Ida, she is so happy and really feels the worst days are over. She can only get better," Emma said with a grin and watched as Ida's lip wobbled slightly before letting out the laughter she'd been trying so hard to control. It was so unexpected and infectious that Emma couldn't resist joining her.

"I'm going to have to get my own dinner myself from now on," Ida finally said, holding her side as she returned to the apartment.

Emma entered her apartment unit, still grinning from the conversation with Ida.

Sometimes Ida could be totally unpredictable and do something out of her character. It was usually hilarious when she did.

"Hey, darling," Robert called from the recliner and got up to enfold her in a hug.

"You are home early today, baby. That is so surprising," Emma said curiously and tried to pull him closer, but he moved away and returned to sit on the recliner.

“Anything wrong?”

Robert shrugged and commented, “You smell of red wine. Took a detour from work?”

Emma laughed gaily, throwing her hands up in the air as she flung her bag on the mahogany table and went to straddle her husband. A mysterious smile rested on her lips.

“Guess who won best columnist of the week award?”

Robert's laid-back expression changed suddenly into one of interest, “Tell me. Who?”

“Yours truly,” Emma replied, staring into his eyes.

“That is great news. I'm so proud of you, baby,” Robert said, a touch of pride in his voice.

Emma kissed him. “But there is sad news in all of this.”

“Sad news?”

“Yes, Robert,” she replied, turning to rest her back on his soft comfortable chest. “Dahlia retired today, and we don't know who the next manager will be until tomorrow. Naturally, we assumed it would go to Cliff, her assistant, but it seems like they are bringing in somebody new.”

“That is a great change, you know. I hope the new manager is something like Dahlia,” Robert said close to her ears.

“Me too.”

They drifted into companionable silence, and Emma's thoughts strayed to the new manager and the change she was sure would take place in the agency.

She remembered dinner and called her husband's name repeatedly before his eyes came into focus, and he turned to stare at her.

Emma was disquieted for some seconds and looked closer at his face to see stress lines on his brow and a brewing storm in his eyes. He was trying valiantly to shield it from her.

“Is there something you're not telling me, Robert? I've been calling your name for a while now, and you look pensive.”

He shook his head and fingered a curl of her hair. “Yeah, I remember something I've not told you today. You are beautiful.”

Emma gave a short smile. “Thank you, Robert, but that's not the answer I'm looking for. Talk to me, baby. Is it work?”

Robert remained silent and Emma pressed on.

“Talk to me, will you?“

“No, peaches. I told you everything is okay. Don't worry your precious head about me. How about we order our favorite pepperoni and cheese pizza with some wings tonight?” Robert asked and kissed her.

Emma broke the kiss and stared at him for a long moment before nodding. “Okay, let’s do that. I'm literally exhausted, too.”

Robert lifted her, as usual, and placed her on the recliner. “Sit tight. Let me make the call.”

Frowning, Emma watched him leave. *Something is definitely not right*, she pondered to herself.

Robert was usually gregariously happy when he returned in the evenings. Or even when he appeared tired or tense, he shrugged out of it quickly in the course of time.

Perhaps they'd been spending too much time apart and had being ignoring their usual traditions. Emma and Robert had made quite a few traditions in almost a year of their marriage. The first was three years prior to their wedding, when they were still dating.

During the weekends before Christmas, the pair of them would fill two hot-and-cold mugs of hot chocolate and pack some baked cookies in warm food flasks. Then they would get into the car and turn on some Christmas tunes, driving through the streets to gaze at the Christmas lights and beautiful houses already decorated for Christmas.

More often than not, the Christmas sightseeing usually switched from just looking at decorations to pointing out houses they'd like to live in and neighborhoods that would be perfect to raise a family. On the ride back home, they would talk about their dream home and the kind of decorations they'd put up before inviting their family and friends over for celebrations and Christmas dinner.

Emma and Robert shared one special thing in common; their love for Christmas.

They acted incredibly sweet, like little kids during Christmas, and everyone around them would sigh in wistfulness.

Emma enjoyed those days when they would recline in front of the TV and watch reruns of classic Christmas movies with the fire crackling and their feet encased in thick wooly stockings, sipping hot cocoa.

She also missed their weekend picnic at the Botanical Gardens from where they'd take a long drive through the city with their windows down, enjoying the scenery.

Sunday mornings were spent in Church. After which they grabbed a quick brunch at the Ten Mile house down on Fifth Avenue. They’d return home to spend the rest of the day in companionable silence with Emma finishing last minute details on work, and Robert watching a morning taped show of the Red Sox games.

Emma missed their weekends together.

Lately, their workloads had increased with the holidays drawing closer and the year wrapping up with alarming speed. Robert was incredibly busy with the airline as lots of people came in and went out of the state. Emma had also taken up an extra column because they needed the additional income as demands of things had skyrocketed and prices were horribly inflated.

Emma promised to make sure they spent the weekend together; work and other activities put aside so they could connect with each other again. Nothing should come between the two of them, she decided and went to find her husband.

CHAPTER 4

Emma sighed dreamily as she walked down Michigan Avenue. Everywhere she turned, the sound of Christmas carols and jingling bells at the entrance of shops enveloped her like a soothing hug. Her cheeks were heavily flushed. She tightened her coat and inhaled the cold biting breeze of the November evening.

Chicago was beautiful at this time of year. After the huge flair of Halloween, the pumpkins and costumes disappeared and were replaced almost immediately by ornaments and sparkles.

Emma loved the Miles more during the holidays and avoided taking the train from her office. She preferred to walk down Michigan Avenue, admiring the wrapped presents and decorated trees displayed by the windows.

Starting from the sixth of November, the Magnificent Miles light festival began. It was usually followed with a huge parade and fireworks over the Chicago River at North Michigan Avenue. Emma and Robert never missed any of it.

Hurrying into the cafe where her friends were waiting for their last book club meeting of the year, Emma couldn't help her thoughts from drifting to Robert.

Her mother had always told her she possessed a sharp instinct; those instincts were never to be disregarded even in faint moments.

Those same instincts were telling Emma that things didn't seem right with Robert.

“Hey, girl, over here!” She heard Susie Ann call.

Emma shoved the niggling worry down and looked up to see the girls sitting by a different alcove from where they usually sat.

“Em, darling, you looked lost there for a second. Are you alright?” Lynn asked, looking her over.

Emma pasted on a cheery smile, pulled off her coat and sat down, but avoided Lynn's eyes. “No, girls, I’m not lost. Sorry, I'm late, though. I walked from the office. “

Lynn was the most perceptive person Emma had ever met. She had the ability to sense when something was wrong and never backed down until she had it all out in the open. They'd been roommates at college, and amongst all her friends, Lynn was the one who knew her best.

“And I'm sure you spent more of the time standing and staring into the shops,” Jessica teased.

“You forgot to mention exclaiming at every shiny bauble and little Santa,” Susie Ann added with a laugh.

Emma grinned. “The whole city is transforming into a wonderland, and it's really beautiful. You guys are just Scrooges. Really!”

“I’d better remain a Scrooge than turn into you at Christmas, Emma,” Lynn finally spoke after watching Emma closely for a minute. “Remember that year in college when you made me walk almost a mile because you were searching for a particular ornament? You were terrible, Emma.”

Everyone collapsed in laughter while Emma shrugged. “In my defense, guys, it was quite a beautiful ornament. If I’d left everything to Lynn, we wouldn't have any decorations at all.”

Jessica went into a huge story about a Christmas incident at Wisconsin with her husband's folks which kept them in fits of giggles. Before long, the group had drifted into talk of families and where they would be spending Christmas.

An hour later, Emma sat beside Lynn who'd offered to drive her home. They lived minutes away from each other and saw each other more often than the others.

"You know I mean to pry, so I won't bother saying I don't. You seemed a lot off in there. Anything wrong?"

Emma began to shake her head when Lynn cut her off quickly

"I won't take no for an answer. I've known you longer than that, Em."

"I'm just worried about Robert," Emma finally said staring out into the road. "It's nothing really. But I feel something is off lately, and he is not telling me."

Lynn patted her hand. "I'm sure it's nothing serious, or he probably would have."

Emma sat up and nodded. "Yes, he probably would have. I think I'm just reading too much into everything."

"When aren't you?" Lynn teased, and Emma swatted her on the shoulder and laughed. Her mood was much better by the time they arrived at her house.

Lynn always did that to her.

Time seemed to stop as Lydia Stone walked into the agency on Wednesday morning.

She was tall and slender with beautiful honey blonde hair cut in a playful pageboy style.

That was where all the softness ended abruptly.

From the dark blue suit, to the stern formidable look she wore, Emma felt uneasy as they were summoned for a quick meeting in the conference room.

Everyone was there, including the freelancers, the travel reporters and publishers.

Emma could feel collective winces around the room when she flung the previous day's paper on the table with a flick of her wrist.

“This is not cutting it,” she said, her tone sharp and as frosty as icicles.

“I will be making lots of changes around here, and unfortunately have to let some people go. The agency is operating on a shoestring budget as it is, so the paper’s content is not exactly stimulating or garnering enough attention.”

The silence that descended after the announcement was so deep that every shallow breath could was heard.

Everybody shuffled uncomfortably, and Emma could tell what was going through their heads.

After the meeting was over, and everyone had returned to their cubicle, Emma was summoned into Lydia's office.

She walked in and took the seat Lydia offered, trying hard to calm her nerves.

“Hi, Emma. I've heard so much about you.”

Emma met the other woman's cold stare with surprise and mixed feelings. She didn't know what to say.

“I've gone through your column avidly, and I must say it’s quite a hit.”

Emma smiled with relief and thanked her in a rushed breath. She'd been thinking of the worst.

“I will need you to be more than a hit,” Lydia continued briskly. “I want you to come up with something really good for the holiday. Something uplifting but a little more controversial.”

“Alright, Ma'am,” Emma replied, nodding with enthusiasm.

“I want to have a draft of it in a fortnight,” Lydia said and dismissed her.

Immediately, Emma left the office. She heaved a sigh of relief and headed for her cubicle but was cornered instantly by Caroline who had a familiar gleam in her eyes.

“What was that all about? Let me have it.”

“I'm so relieved. I thought I was getting the sack,” Emma replied as she slung into her chair.

“Then what was it?” She asked, motioning frantically. “Tell me! Stop hoarding important news,” Caroline chided.

“She commended my column. I guess she's been following it for a while.”

“And?”

“She wants me to come up with something big for Christmas. A series to run for the entire holiday,” Emma admitted.

Caroline's face fell. “It sounded ominous. I really thought you were getting laid off.”

Emma blinked in surprise. “You look awfully happy about that possibility.”

“Why would you say such a thing! I am just concerned about you, Emma,” Caroline said, looking offended. “I'll talk to you when you aren't feeling so judgmental.”

Emma watched her walk off in a tiff and wondered what Caroline's true intentions were. Sometimes she acted genuinely concerned about her, but most often, she looked secretly pleased things weren't exactly kosher with her.

Like the time Emma made the mistake of speaking about a little fight she'd had with Robert. Caroline had murmured the right words and calmed her. But the next day, Emma overhead two female reporters in the restroom gossiping about how 'not so perfect' her marriage was.

Emma wasn't close to anyone in the office except Caroline and despite her overtly friendly personality, she didn't believe in discussing her private life with just anyone. She hadn't known how to confront Caroline about the issue, so she kept it to herself but refrained from that point on from discussing anything but work-related issues.

Emma shrugged off thoughts about Caroline and faced her laptop. She had to come up with an idea fast before the fierce Lydia Stone came down on her.

She couldn't afford to be out of a job anytime soon, especially before Christmas.

***

Robert was in a foul mood. He paced the entire length of the living room, willing his phone to ring. He'd been calling Emma for the past hour, but she wasn't picking up.

The doorbell rang, so he strode to the door to give her a good talking to but Emma wasn't on the other side. Ingrid Baker, one of the old ladies from the first floor, was in a purple frumpy dress and the weirdest Christmas hat Robert had ever seen.

"Hi dear," she said warmly despite the scowl on his face. "Is Emma home yet?"

"No, she isn't. I will let her know you called once she gets back," Robert said through gritted teeth. Emma was still out although it was ten p.m. and wasn't answering her phone.

Ingrid hobbled nervously for some seconds before she nodded and left.

Robert berated himself. He knew he was acting out of character, but he didn't care. There was just too much on his mind, and he'd only wanted to come home and eat dinner then brood by the TV.

He heard the doorknob again almost an hour later but sat silently fuming on the couch.

"Hi, honey," Emma said, as she juggled two boxes of Chinese takeout and her bag. She pushed the door shut with her hip.

"Sorry I'm late and couldn't take my calls. Today has been pure hell."

Robert turned his face away as she leaned down to kiss him.

"I'm sorry, Robbie," She crooned and tried to take his face in her hands but stopped when she noted his angry glare.

"You should have tried to answer your phone just once. My job is stressful, too, you know, but I always try to leave you little texts every time I can. It's not wrong to expect more from you!" He snapped.

Emma flinched and drew back, regarding him with a frown. "I have been pretty busy. My new boss is sterner and a bit more demanding..."

"It's not always about you, Emma!" Robert shouted, cutting her off.

Emma stood in the middle of the living room, mouth gaping open. "That was terribly uncalled for, Robert. I don't know what has got you. You've been unsettled for some days now, but you shouldn't have said that. You know I always try to reach you during the day. Matter of fact, you've been behaving a lot stranger lately."

Robert stiffened, feeling like a heel at the hurt on her face and called himself a fool. He moved to take her hand, but she walked toward the bedroom.

"I'm sorry, Emma," Robert followed behind her. He couldn't believe he'd gone off like that.

Guilt ripped his chest, as he approached his wife who stood by the window. She was silently staring at the snowfall.

"Will you please forgive me, honey? I had no basis for the nonsense I just spouted."

Emma turned to stare at him. Concern settled on her face as she said, "There is something not quite right, Robert. I know because you only lash out like this when something is terribly wrong."

Robert ran his hands through his hair and sighed heavily. "Come here, my love."

Emma moved reluctantly into his outstretched arms, and he pulled her into a tight hug.

"I'm sorry for being such an idiot. You know you mean the world to me, baby," He said gently, nuzzling his nose into her hair.

"I think we should talk. We've not been spending that much time together," Emma said and snuggled closer to his chest.

Robert drew back, framing her face. "Yes, we need to talk, but it's about something else entirely."

Emma took his hand and led him to the four-poster mahogany bed they'd found on an exclusive flea market bargain sale.

"I have to quit my job."

"Your job?"

He nodded solemnly, wincing at the shock etched on her face.

“What! Why would you do that, Robbie? Have you gotten another job offer?”

Robert sighed. “I can't work at Southwest Airlines anymore. I have to find something else before Christmas, probably at another airline.”

“This is so sudden. Why do you have to quit? I know the job is harder and tougher during the holiday season, but I thought the airline was doing considerably well,” Emma said, unable to keep the alarm out of her voice.

“It's not about the airline, Emma.”

“Then talk to me! I don't understand any of this, “Emma said a little too sharply.

“There is a situation at work,” Robert began, his scowl deepening. He told his anxious wife all about his boss and the illegal runs.

He was in a tight spot. If he made the mistake of doing the right thing and going to the overall directors, then he stood to be the fall guy for his ruthless boss. Richard wasn't someone who bluffed.

“Then you stay and keep quiet, Robert!” He heard his wife say after he was done explaining the precarious position he'd found himself in. He stared at her, unable to believe she’d just said that.

“Could you be clearer, Emma? What do you mean by that?”

She shook her head, eyes wide as she repeated, “You keep your job and keep the information to yourself is what I mean. It's almost Christmas. There is no chance you'd get another one easily.”

“You must me kidding me, Emma. Do you realize what you just said right now?” Robert said, after a few seconds of shocked silence.

Emma stood and began to pace the room, her eyes glittering. “You don't have to be so freaking moral all the time, Robert. It’s none of your business really. Just keep your mouth shut, do your job, and get paid. You remember how hard it was to get this job while you took night classes.”

“I've known you for a long time and love you each passing day, but I cannot believe you right now,” Robert said icily. “This has been on my mind constantly, Emma. You expect me to keep working with him as an accessory just to keep my job?”

“No one is asking you to be an accessory, Rob, no one! Just stay out of his way. Sooner or later, he'll get caught and it won't be at your detriment, darling,” She said, her voice growing soft. She came to put her arms around his neck, but with his jaw clenched in anger, Robert moved away.

He couldn't believe Emma would say such a thing. She was such a stickler for rules and morals and taught the little kids at Sunday school all about it.

“Come on, Robert. I know this doesn't sound like the right thing to do, but you know how things are at the moment. We can barely afford extravagances as it is. We have to live strictly by a budget. I have to come up with something big for Christmas, or I might be out of a job too,” Emma implored.

“Because we need extra income, you’re telling me we should let this slide? Go against things we believe strongly in?” Robert asked her quietly

Emma tried to speak but stopped halfway and just stood there, staring at him.

He was disappointed and lost for words too. Instead of giving his tongue the chance to say anything hurtful, Robert chose to leave the house and go for a long walk.

It had stopped snowing some minutes ago, but the sharp biting cold would do him a world of good. He needed to assemble his thoughts and make the right decisions despite the growing frustration that threatened to drag him under.

CHAPTER 5

Emma stirred groggily from sleep and turned to peer at the bedside clock. With a yelp, she jumped out of bed and stumbled as her feet got tangled in the covers. Muttering something incoherent, she rushed into the bathroom for a quick shower.

The Christmas *Fix It by Emma* draft was due this morning, and now she'd be late. She would appear tardy to her new boss, which wasn't the image she was striving for at this particular moment.

The house was empty, but Emma found a note lying on the kitchen table, as she brewed a quick cup of coffee. A heavy sigh left her as her shoulders sagged. Robert had taken to leaving her a note when he left very early in the mornings for days now after their fight. He didn't send her his usual quirky text messages during the day anymore and barely made it in time for dinner.

Emma felt suddenly angry and tossed the note in the waste bin. He was just so hardheaded and annoyingly pragmatic sometimes.

How could keeping quiet and staying out of that corrupt business be a bad thing? She'd been drawn to his strong will, especially concerning matters of principle, but at the moment, those wouldn't help pay the bills or keep his job.

Emma couldn't see how hard it would be to just do his job and overlook whatever wasn't his business. She rinsed out her coffee cup in the sink after a quick gulp and hurried to gather the notes scattered on the bedside table. Then she rushed out of the apartment. If she had to call a cab, she would to get to the office and save some time.

Her phone rang just as she got down from the stairs. It was her mother.

"Hi, Mom!" she said, answering on the third ring and waved to Mr. Stuart from the bookstore across the street. Emma opted to flag down a cab instead since she couldn't call them while on the phone to her mother.

"Em, darling... How are you this morning?" Her mother's cheery voice reached through the lines to draw her into a familiar embrace.

"I'm okay, Mom. On my way to the office, though. How are you and Dad?"

"Just fine," her mother replied with a laugh. "Your father just took up playing golf, and my, he looks real uncomfortable holding the stick like it's the book of life."

Emma giggled, "I can just picture him standing there with a fierce look in his eyes like a soldier going off to war."

"Ha! You should see him. Now he tells me he has more important things to think about like beating Norman, the highest player at the golf club, and rising to the ranks of Tiger Woods."

Emma couldn't stop the laughter that spilled out of her, as she hefted her bag on her shoulders and walked down the street to flag down her ride. "Dad is hilarious. Good luck to him then. I will give him a call later to congratulate him properly. I can't wait to be recognized as the daughter of a popular golfer."

Her mother's unrestrained tinkling laughter filled Emma with a smile, as she settled in the back of the taxi and gave the driver directions.

"Dear, I have a meeting on Michigan Avenue this morning. I'm sure it will run for a while, but would you be free to meet up for lunch?" Her mother asked hopefully.

Emma's thoughts raced in a million directions. It all depended on Lydia's verdict on the draft. If it didn't meet her expectations, she'd have to spend the entirety of lunch break redoing it till it was perfect.

"Mom, I'll have to call you back about that when I get to the office. There is so much happening right now that I want to talk to you about."

"Okay, darling. Talk to you soon," her mother replied and blew her a kiss before ending the call.

Emma smiled at the phone. She'd missed talking to her Mom and lunch would be a perfect time to catch up.

Her parents lived just thirty minutes away from Evanston in Lake Forest; a city in Lake County, Illinois. The schedules of her job and Robert's didn't give them much time to drive out to visit as regularly as they would have wanted.

Emma's father was a retired banker who spent most of his time trying out new ways to keep from being bored from retirement, and her mother ran a pet care store in which Emma had spent the majority of her teenage years working. She'd been surrounded by a lot of dogs, cats, and birds growing up and, on some occasions, iguanas and hamsters.

The apartment she lived in with Robert didn't allow pets. Emma couldn't wait for their own home so she could buy a dog and maybe a cat.

***

In all his time working as a ramper for Southwest airlines, Robert had never been inside the office of the management. As he stood waiting for Harry Donovan, the chief operating officer for Southwest Airlines at O'Hare, Robert wondered why he'd been summoned.

He'd spoken to the enigmatic man once when he'd travelled to Michigan to work on a special assignment with Richard. Harry had commented on his efficiency and dedication on the ramp and gave him a hundred dollar tip.

He rarely saw him at O'Hare since he mostly hung out on the ramp or in the employee lounge. He hadn't known the man recognized or knew his name.

The directors didn't concern themselves with the ramp agents or baggage boys, as they were popularly called. Besides, Michigan had been a long time ago.

As Robert stood in the reception, his heartbeat nervously in his chest, and he muttered a quick prayer.

He hadn't told anyone anything, not even when Bill Hunter and Wes Tucker had asked him what his reasons were for quitting. He hadn't said a word. After days of battling with his moral compass and worrying about going back to the job market again, Robert had finally decided to quit his job.

He'd considered going to the HR manager and discreetly mentioning the security of loading baggage on the planes and double checks for illegal smuggled items after the airport agents were done searching, but he knew that would only cause a backlash. Richard had lots of loyal acquaintances and friends in the airline. Whatever he did could cause issues with their jobs, too.

The risk involved was too great. Robert had no extra money to pay employment lawyers or go to court. Quitting the job was the only viable option to keep his morals intact and avoid being the victim of a very unscrupulous man.

When he came to the final decision to leave, a blissful calm had settled over his shoulders, easing the knots of worry that had taken up residence there for almost a week now.

He knew Emma had only said the words she did because she loved him and didn't want to see him struggle for another job at the end of the year.

He had a plus on his side though. Ramp agencies favored people who were physical and brawny, and he was sure it wouldn't take long before he got another job at a different airline.

O'Hare airport had over ninety airlines and also because it was the end of the year, the demands for ramp agents would be quite high.

The only downside was the influx of employees that had quadrupled in the past months, but Robert was positive he would get a job soon and he trusted God.

“Robert McAllister.”

Robert turned and stood up hurriedly as the director crossed the gap between them to take his hand.

“Good afternoon, sir,” Robert said with a bravado he wasn't feeling. His thoughts were jumbled up in an unpleasant disarray.

“I happened to be taking a call when I overhead some rampers and ticket agents talking about your sudden resignation. They said it seemed like a spur of the moment decision. We happened to have recently increased the paycheck, so it seemed puzzling to me. So, which is it?”

Robert was speechless. He stared at the director for a few short seconds. He couldn't believe the man remembered him.

“It's complicated. I can't talk about my reasons, but God has a special plan for us and it's for the best,” he said hurriedly to make up for the uncomfortable lapse of silence.

The director was silent for a while with an unreadable expression on his face. “He does work in mysterious ways, doesn't he?"

Robert stared straight into the man's eyes and knew he understood. He might not know the whole details, but he knew this was something Robert had to do.

"Well, good luck then," he said and turned to leave.

Robert sighed with relief. His legs felt like jelly as he walked out of the office. He'd been so worried Richard had done what he threatened and turned the noose onto him.

He walked out of the airport and into the afternoon sun like a man who'd been relieved of a large and heavy load.

The opportunity to tell the director everything about Richard and his underground dealings had been there. He knew there was a chance the man would've believed him. Richard was away in Ohio, so he wasn't there to engineer the incident which would have incriminated him.

But Robert also knew the stark cold truth. Things weren't just black or white. Richard would have taken measures to protect himself. From the moment Robert had caught him in the act, he was afraid that Richard would retaliate. He just knew he was the type of man who covered his tracks.

Besides, it wasn't his sin to tell. He knew soon enough that Richard would slip and face the penalty for his actions. Robert had done the best thing he could do in the situation to save himself and still not compromise what he believed in.

As he got into the car and turned on the ignition, Robert thought of his wife. He understood Emma only wanted what was best for him and it'd all come from a deep well of love and concern.

He'd missed talking to her these past few days and knew Emma could get a lot adamant and unyielding when she had an idea in her head about something. Robert had fallen in love with that fierce determination.

Weaving through the afternoon traffic, Robert thought of the best way to apologize to her. An idea popped into his head, and he struggled to hold back the laughter.

He was going to cook for her and not his usual fare of bacon and eggs or pancakes which he made most Saturday mornings and served her in bed. He would try his hand at cooking something slightly different and more complicated.

As Robert made for the grocery store, he couldn't help the wide grin that stuck to his face. He parked carefully and turned off the engine to search through Google for a simple exotic meal and wasn't disappointed. There was a load of varieties to choose from.

He kept on grinning from ear to ear as he scrolled through, wincing at some bizarre looking meals with weird names. He finally settled on a one pot exotic pasta with chicken and sausages. It looked good enough and the directions were quite easy to follow. He couldn't wait to see the look on Emma's face when she returned home to the surprise meal.

Robert hoped it would turn out well and taste as good as it looked. He made a mental note to put the Pizza Place on speed dial in case things didn't turn out as planned.

CHAPTER 6

Emma fidgeted nervously as she watched Lydia flip through the pages of the *Fix It by Emma* Christmas draft with no expression on her face.

After some seconds, she flipped it closed and tossed it on the table towards Emma.

"Brilliant, Emma. It was actually good."

"Thank you," Emma answered politely, thumping down the urge to break into a rendition of 'Alleluia'. She'd been incredibly nervous to present the draft since she got to the office. Rebecca from reception had whispered to her when she came in to keep her head. Lydia had fired two reporters and a columnist and seemed to be in a snit that morning.

From the moment she stepped into the office, her palms had been sweaty as Lydia wore the coldest look Emma had ever seen.

"Now listen, Emma, I won't say this twice." Lydia began, leveling a frosty stare at her. "I don't know how your previous boss ran this ship, or the free rein she let you all have but it ends here. I don't do favoritism or mollycoddling. I don't want baked cookies or after-work coffees. I just want you to do your job and do it well. Are we on the same page?"

"Yes, ma'am," Emma nodded, keeping a straight face despite the rising turmoil and anger brewing inside her.

"Prepare for the first publication. You don't have any slot for Thanksgiving, use the time to work on the first of December and send it to me."

Emma nodded, meeting the woman's unblinking stare before picking up the draft to walk out of the office.

It wasn't until she got to her cubicle that Emma allowed herself to release the pent-up breath and furious groan that she'd held back for the last fifteen minutes.

Dahlia had been the best boss anyone could have asked for and had never showed favoritism. She gave every journalist in the press their due credit and a listening ear and rewarded them with praise for every milestone they crossed. Dahlia was just a very friendly woman who got involved with her employees on a personal level but still never hesitated to come down hard on them when they erred.

Emma knew Lydia had done her investigations in the press or got her information from someone within the press who hadn't been pleased by the situation. Her mind quickly went to Caroline, and she shot the preposterous idea down. Caroline had some issues, but she wouldn't deliberately cause unrest within the agency. Emma sighed heavily and closed her eyes to pray for strength and ask for forgiveness for her judgmental thoughts.

***

"Mom! You restyled your hair!" Emma sauntered up to her mother with a beaming smile on her face. She was seated by a window of the restaurant.

"You like it? Winona did hers too. It made her look years younger, so I decided to give it a try." Her mother stood to enfold her in a hug.

Emma grinned at her mother who didn't look a day over fifty. "It's beautiful. I love it, Mom."

"Yeah?" she scoffed. "Your father said I did it to make him appear way older. Says he feels like a grandpa standing close to me these days."

Emma laughed. Her father could be such a hoot sometimes.

He was always at the receiving end when she teamed up with her mother. She wanted to be as happy as they were together with Robert when they got older.

Her mother looked calm and regal with her newly styled brunette bob mixed with gray strands which gave character to her electric blue eyes and serene smile. Emma missed those smiles, and their ability to put one at ease with themselves.

“Are you okay, Emma? You seem to have taken a trip there for a second. Everything alright, baby?” Her mother asked with a worried frown and turned to wave the hovering waitress off with an apology.

Emma shook her head and smiled a little too brightly. She wondered if its falseness was glaringly obvious. “I'm fine Mom. How did your meeting go?”

“Really well. I have to wait for a phone call to confirm the state of things, but it’ll get all sorted out.” Her mother was still giving her probing looks. “You know, peaches, you don't know a thing about keeping secrets. One look and it's all magnificently laid out to see.”

Emma beckoned the waitress over and ordered a tall cup of cappuccino. Her mother's cup of tea sat untouched while she waited for Emma to quit stalling.

After taking a long swallow, Emma finally turned to her. “Mom, stop giving me the 'I'll be here when you are ready' face. There is nothing except for the new boss and the tense workspace.”

“You mentioned that. Tell me all about it. What is she like?” Her mother asked and took a small sip of her tea.

“She is really tough. Strictly professional and cold. She's fired three people already, Mom!”

Emma's mother winced. “In a space of days? How are you holding up? Everyone is bound to be tense with that going on.”

Emma shook her head. “You don't know how much tension is constantly hovering around everyone. She has wonderful ideas that will boost the agency, but she's cutting out almost everything else that made us a personal, unique press. We’ve always been close-knit with our readers.”

Her mother patted her hand gently. “I'm sure it will get better eventually. She’ll realize how wonderful everyone in the press is and how it feels like family. Maybe she won’t tamper with it too much.”

Emma took a sip of her cappuccino and shrugged. “I think she's misguided, and that there are people deliberately poisoning her mind.”

Her mother blanched. “Really! Why would anyone in the agency do that?”

“Same thing I've been asking myself, Mom.” Emma looked outside to smile at a couple kissing by the sidewalk.

She missed Robert so much and wished she could tell him about her new boss and the situation at the office. She missed waking up to him puttering around the house mumbling about where everything was.

“Emma, dear, I asked how Robert is doing. You seem incredibly distracted. Are you sure it's just work? You haven’t mentioned Robert since you got here.”

Emma turned to frown at her mother. “You are too perceptive, Mom. Trying to hide anything from you is frustrating.”

“And you are too expressive, Em. It’s written all over you,” she replied with a knowing smile. “You've been out of sorts since you stepped in here. You have not taken more than two sips of that cappuccino or kept your brows from furrowing together. It can't just be work stressing you out so badly."

Emma sighed heavily and admitted, "Mom, it's Robert. I don't know if I handled the situation properly, or I just messed it all up."

Her mother kept quiet but arched a brow.

"Robert has a situation at work. His supervisor is involved in something illegal underground and threatening Robert if he says anything about it. He'd lose his job or, worse yet, be framed for the crime," Emma whispered. Her mom gasped and her eyes went wide.

"What is it all about? This is really bad! Do we need to get a lawyer? "

"He wants to resign because he claims it's the only way to avoid following along with it. He's afraid of being framed or remaining there, maybe being messed up with it somehow, " Emma said a little too sharply.

"And what do you think of all this, Emma? The situation is threatening and horrible. It should be handled as such. What do you think he should do? "Her mother asked, both eyebrows climbing even higher.

Emma shrugged and looked away. "It's the end of the year. Finding another job might not be too easy. Plus, overlooking the whole thing and doing his part of the job won't make him less moral. At least that's what I think."

"Emma, how can you say that?!"

"Mom, I know it sounds wrong and horrible, but I don't want him to be out of a job at this time of year. We are really trying to find our foothold. I can't stand seeing him stressed out, but I don't want to either of us to struggle financially," Emma said unhappily, her voice breaking in the middle.

Her mother grasped her palm and squeezed it. “I know, Em, I know how it is. You care for him deeply.” She tugged her palm gently until Emma was looking her in the eyes. “Can I ask you an important question, dear?”

Emma nodded after a few seconds, trying to hold back tears.

“Would you have married Robert if you knew he was that sort of person?”

Emma was at a loss for words. She stared at her mother, thinking back to all the things she loved about Robert. Tears filled her eyes as she shook her head. “Oh, Mom, I've been a fool!”

Maude squeezed her hand tighter and disagreed with her. “Not a fool, Em. You only thought what you felt was best.”

“Of course, I wouldn't marry that kind of person,” Emma went on, guilt eating her up inside.

“He’ll understand. Don't be too hard on yourself. Talk to him and apologize.”

Emma felt like laughing at herself. She'd been disagreeable with him, yet he’d needed her to understand. She hadn’t understood why he’d been angry with her for a decision that hadn't been right; something she would have condemned about someone else. She'd let their need for financial security push her into encouraging him to do something that was really wrong and unlawful.

She had to talk to Robert and apologize to him immediately. Emma was suddenly in a hurry to get home.

“Mom, thank you very much. What would I do without you?” She asked.

Smiling, her mother raised her hands, palm up. “Yeah, I know you love me. Hurry home. Alright!”

Emma couldn't hide a grin as she bent to kiss her mother's cheek.

“Don't forget to come help prepare for thanksgiving quite early. Robert needs to bring a bottle of wine and his full attention to hear your father brag all about his newfound golf prowess.”

“Yes, ma'am. Noted,” Emma replied with a laugh and grabbed her mother in a tight hug. “Thank you, Mom, really.”

“Just doing my job. It has absolutely nothing to do with the fact that I love your cute face,” her mother teased and kissed her cheek.

Emma walked with her mother to the car and watched till she drove off before walking a little too fast to the office.

She had a plan. She would drop in at the little grocery store after work and pick up some wings and salad dressing.

She would try to finish up in time to make it home before he did; pop the wings in the pan, take a luxurious bath and wear something nice. If she had to apologize till her face turned blue, she would, but she knew Robert would never let it get to that. He probably would make a joke about not thinking a blue-faced, long-term wife was going to be a good thing.

Emma smiled as she stepped into the office lobby. Tonight, she would forget all about work pressures or deadlines or anything else. She would only concern herself with being wrapped up in her husband's arm and listen to his heart beating through his shirt.

CHAPTER 7

Emma stared at the screen of her laptop in dismay, willing the rapid mumbo jumbo to stop marching across her screen. Panicking, she yanked out the flash drive with her files. The laptop shut down instantly.

"This is not happening," she muttered and tapped the power button. The screen remained black. She hit it again and repeated, "This can't be happening." Her computer wasn't coming on at all.

Emma bit back a scream. Before leaving for lunch with her mother, she'd turned off the laptop and left her flash drive in it. She didn't understand what was happening right now.

She snapped it shut and took it to the IT room. "Marcus, I need your help right now. I'm freaking scared." She said to the tall ginger-haired young man sitting and typing briskly on the laptop in front of him.

"Emma, I'm incredibly busy right now. Could—"

"Something's wrong with my laptop, and I need to retrieve my files before it's too late!" Emma cut in, pleading with her eyes at the tech guy who was looking unusually harried.

She knew everyone was tense, but what else was she going to do?

He finally gave in after a few seconds of disgruntled mumblings. "What is wrong with it? And when did you notice?"

Emma hovered close to him and told him how she had inserted the flash drive into her laptop and it rebooted again, showing a bunch of weird codes before it went off and refused to come on again.

Marcus asked her a series of questions while he worked on her laptop. He requested for the flash and inserted it on the desktop to perform a scan. He spoke up after a couple of minutes. “Your flash drive is corrupted with a virus, Emma.”

“A virus?! But that's impossible. I worked with it before leaving for lunch, and it was just fine. I haven’t used it on any other device since then,” Emma rung her hands and fought the stinging in her eyes. How and when did her flash drive get corrupted?

Marcus stopped for a beat and asked, puzzled. “But don't you have an antivirus installed on your laptop for protection?”

“I do. That’s right! Why is this happening?” Pacing the small length of the agency's tech room, Emma couldn’t stop shaking.

Marcus whistled as he finally powered the system on and turned to Emma. “Okay. The virus is not a complicated one. If it had been left for a longer period before you'd brought it in here, maybe we’d have issues. But for now, you have nothing to worry about. I will try to recover your files, but it will take me until tomorrow. I have too much to do, and have you met our new boss?” He glanced her way and grimaced. “Judging by that look, you have.”

Emma was barely holding back a flood of panic. “Tomorrow is Saturday. How would I get it? You won't be here.”

Marcus frowned. “Uh, see there’s the thing. I will be here. We all work Saturdays from now on.” His tone was bitter as he turned back to the laptop.

“I'm sorry. At least you get off earlier. That's a little consolation, I guess. It's better than nothing, isn't it?” Emma asked, then looked up from the floor to see him staring at her.

“Riiight.” He didn’t look the least consoled.

“Well, thank you, Marcus. I'll have to use a loaned one before tomorrow. Thank you very much!” She gushed and left him with a shoulder squeeze and a bright red face.

***

Emma hurried to the apartment with a smile and worry over her laptop. Now she'd suffer a delay getting her piece written and extra coldness from her new boss.

With so much on her mind, she bought a cute little Santa with a raised brow while shopping for dinner. She didn't even remember putting it in her basket. In line at the cashier station, she picked it up and smiled.

The brow reminded her of Robert whenever he was teasing her. No wonder she'd picked it out. She paid for everything in record time when it was her turn. In the cab ride home, she debated calling him but decided against it. She would rather face him while she spoke to him.

She stopped in front of Ingrid and Ida's flat and thought of knocking. She hadn't had time to practice the recipe because she had been incredibly busy.

A pleasant yet burning smell greeted Emma as she entered the apartment. She heard Robert singing in the kitchen and wondered what was happening. Shrugging off her coat, she dumped her bag on the couch and carried the groceries into the kitchen.

Emma stifled a laugh. Robert stood by the cooker, an apron tied around his waist, and he was surrounded by a chaotic array of chopped vegetables, pasta, cheese and herb shakers.

He turned to greet her with a smile. "Hi, honey. I thought I should surprise you with a fabulous meal. I found it online."

"Online?" Emma asked gently, her heart blossoming with love. Richard smiled, no sign of the frown he'd worn for a couple of days.

"Yes. I thought it would go great for dinner. Just in case, the

Pizza Place delivers anytime." He grinned wider.

"I had the same idea, too." Emma chuckled. "I stopped by to get some wings and salad dressings. You beat me to it though. What is this called? It looks like it might be burnings" She said, sniffing the air.

"Exotic pasta with chicken and sausage. It smells and looks heavenly. Let's hope it tastes the same." Robert turned to the pan of pasta, sausage, chicken and cheese and stirred. "It can't be burning. It hasn't been on for the recommended length of time yet."

Emma smiled and shook her head. She reached around him and turned down the heat on the cooker.

Robert bent to kiss her lips, dropping the potholder as he took her in his arms. Emma was almost giddy. She opened her mouth to speak, but Robert cut her off.

"I'm sorry, darling. I've missed you so much. I let my anger get the best of me," he said regrettably, caressing her face with his thumb.

Emma shook her head and cupped his face in her hands, just like she'd been yearning to do since the conversation with her mother and the realization that she'd been wrong all along. "I should be the one apologizing, Rob. I let myself forget for a moment what was right and wrong. I blurred the lines because of selfishness. You are not selfish. I should have been focused on acceptance and how even being around that activity is wrong. I'm so sorry, and I love you beyond words."

Robert shut his eyes tightly for a second and, when he opened them, their depths were filled with intense love. He held her close and kissed her hair. "I love you, Emma. I can't stop loving you, no matter what happens." He drew back to raise her chin with his index finger. "I know you only said that because you didn't want me having any issues, and I love you for that, baby."

Emma stood on tiptoes to kiss him on the lips, feeling the warmth of his skin as he drew her closer.

The strong smell of burning pervaded their senses as they drew apart and Robert turned off the cooker quickly before the rest of the surprise dinner could turn to a blackened mess in the pan.

"I guess we are having burnt pasta tonight, baby," Emma teased, wrapping her arms around Robert from behind as he set the pan of pasta aside to cool. He tried to tidy the kitchen which looked like a disaster zone.

"You know you could stop distracting me, dear wife, and come help me clean up. That would be wondrously appreciated."

"No. I'll let you clean up. You're doing a wonderful job, and I need to take a long shower and treat myself before dinner."

Robert turned and playfully lunged for her, but she side-stepped and ran out of the kitchen. Tonight, felt special. Ever since they had gotten married, they hadn't had a fight that lasted this long. She was glad they had finally resolved it and hadn't let the issue come between them or damage their joy and bliss.

CHAPTER 8

"Good news, Emma. I recovered your documents from the flash drive after a bit of this and that—"

Emma didn't let Marcus finish talking before she squealed and pulled him in for a hug.

"Thank you. Thank you. Thank you, Marcus. You are the best!" She gushed, her curls dancing around her face as she bounced up and down.

"And as I was saying, before you almost squeezed life out of me, I saved it on the computer for you, but you'll have to use a different drive now." Marcus finished off as he struggled to hide his blush.

Emma grinned, barely fazed over his news. "I owe you one, Marcus. Anything I don't have to struggle for. Ha!"

Marcus handed the laptop back to her and said, "If you put it like that... There is something you can do for me that won't require struggling. I think."

Emma gave him a coy smile. "Oh-kay..."

Marcus shifted from one foot to the other. "I see you talking..." He smothered a nervous cough. "I see you talking to Rebecca at the reception desk a lot. You seem to get along well. Am I right?"

"Yeah. We get along pretty good," Emma replied, keeping the excitement of a budding romance out of her voice.

"Well... I was wondering if you would put in a good word or two for me when you're talking to her. I kinda like her. Well, more than kinda. A lot," Marcus finished, looking everywhere but at her.

"Is that all?"

"Yes, Emma... She has this really nice smile. You know? I bet she hasn't even noticed me around," Marcus said, staring off into space.

Emma gave him a mischievous smile. "You never know. Maybe she has noticed and likes you, too. I will offer my two cents worth. Trust me," she said, and grinned as she returned to her cubicle.

Marcus' eyes lit up. She was sure they would remain starry for a while.

Playing matchmaker sounds so delightful, she thought to herself. If it were possible, she wanted everyone she knew to be as deliriously happy as she was with Robert. Falling in love with someone who made your heart sing was the best thing ever. Especially someone who thought the same way as her.

Emma went straight to work and didn't budge until an hour later. She turned to crick her neck and stretch out the stiffness when she felt someone's eyes on her. She turned and caught Caroline's gaze from a few feet across the room. Pure resentment radiated off her and, before Emma looked away, she swore loathing had flashed in those eyes.

Emma returned to her monitor, wanting to discount what she'd seen, but it had been too real and too deep. She cared for Caroline and thought only good things towards her.

Don't go borrowing trouble, Em, observe before you take the wrong step, her mother had told her many times when she was a child.

Emma tried her best to erase negative thoughts. She probably had imagined it all. Caroline was probably looking past Emma, not at her. That had to be it. Besides, why would Carol not like her? She couldn't think of a single reason. Caroline probably had some issues of her own. Emma let it all go and returned to work.

***

Thanksgiving morning was cold and biting as the wind kicked up a fury. Emma was bundled up in a thick wool coat which Lynn had given her last Christmas. It was a brilliant shade of blue and matched the shade of her eyes. Robert said it defined the morning weather perfectly.

"Honey, did you remember to get the wine?" Robert asked.

As she juggled the sack of groceries her mother had requested to the car, she called over shoulder, "No. I have to go back upstairs."

"Don't worry, babe. I'll get it," Robert said and bent to kiss her forehead before setting his own bags in the backseat. "You look beautiful, love."

Emma blushed under Robert's affectionate scrutiny. "You don't look bad yourself."

Robert raised his brows smugly. "Trust me, I know it. Why do you think the prettiest girl I ever met just had to marry me?"

Emma laughed. "You are such a tease. You know that?"

Robert just winked and swaggered off into the apartment. Emma inhaled and looked around. Sighting Ingrid and Ida, she rushed over to them.

"Happy Thanksgiving, ladies. We are looking mighty pretty," she said, admiring the floral dress and pink hat Ingrid wore. Ida had shed her usual drab of black to wear a dove gray gown with a cowed neck, dotted with red and white flowers.

"Thank you, sweetie. Happy Thanksgiving," Ingrid said, preening under the compliment.

"Going off to your folks, are you?" Ida asked as she looked over at Robert who was putting a bottle of wine in the trunk of the car.

"Yes, and we are running late. Mom is very particular," Emma replied and bent to kiss their cheeks. She walked back to the car and waved before getting in.

"Your phone just rang. I think it's your mother," Robert told her.

"Thanks, honey." Emma checked her phone. It was Lydia.

Puzzled, she dialed back immediately, and it connected on the second ring.

"Emma, I would need you to polish off the Christmas story and send it in this afternoon."

"But I sent it yesterday to the print."

"We seem to be having an issue at the press. Most of the articles sent to the print were misplaced. We've recovered everything else except yours. Could you get to it very fast. The papers will be printed shortly," Lydia said briskly and hung up.

"I thought you were done with work for the weekend?" Robert asked.

"It's just strange. The story I sent to the print is missing. I have to resend it right now," Emma replied, a slight frown dotting her face. "I don't get it. I sent it and got a confirmation message. How could it go missing?"

Robert looked away from the road for a second and brushed her face lightly with his palm. "Don't worry, baby, when you get to your folks you can quickly do that. Thank heavens you brought your laptop along."

Emma agreed with Robert instantly and sighed. “But it's all weird, you know? From my flash drive getting a virus and infecting my laptop, whose antivirus protection got disabled, to my story missing. It all seems really weird and direct. “

“Emma...”

Emma turned to Robert who honked before dodging a few cars and turned to her. “Emma, it could be what it is; an accident. Don’t think such thoughts. Besides, who would do that to you? You get along with everyone there.”

Emma debated telling Robert about Caroline but decided against it. No matter how strong the feelings were, those were still mere speculations. Caroline had a Jekyll and Hyde personality, and she, of all people, should have been used to it by now.

“Are you okay, baby? You look confused. Still thinking about it?”

Emma pasted on a smile and rubbed her husband's thigh. “Yes, Mr. McAllister. Who wouldn't be? But I need to focus on taking a Thanksgiving ride with the man I love.”

Robert's eyes warmed and he said softly. “This is our first Thanksgiving as a married couple, Em. It feels good to have you beside me. No matter the issues at the moment, being with you is all that counts.”

“Oh, Robert!” Emma's breath hitched, and her eyes grew moist. “Absolutely. Being with you is the definition of happiness for me.” She leaned over to plant a kiss on his lips as they approached Lake Forest.

***

It was late in the evening before they sat down to dinner. Emma and her mother had been holed up in the kitchen all day while

Robert had taken a ride with her father, Eric, who was intent on showing off his golfing skills. Robert was comfortable with her father who shared a lot of similarities with his own dad. They were both incredible husbands, fathers and devoted Christians who went their own way and never judged anybody.

"I heard about the job and you quitting, son," Eric had said, startling him from his train of thought as they packed the golf equipment and headed off the course to find a ride. Robert nodded and stared straight ahead.

"That was the best decision to make at that point. A quick-witted one, too. Everything could possibly have gone downhill from there. If your boss is the type of person to threaten to set you up, he could do worse than that."

"It was beyond provoking and birthed a desperate idea or two that would have ended disastrously," Robert admitted with a shake of his head. He thanked his restraint in not telling everything to the operating officer. No one knew the state of a man's heart. It could have gone remarkably well, with Richard being investigated and caught in the act. Or with the situation totally manipulated and laid at his doorstep. He knew sooner rather than later things would sort themselves out. His father in-law's next words echoed the thought.

"In such situations, we are often plagued with the heavy dilemma of having to choose between what is extremely wrong, right and in between. It would have been easy to turn a blind eye and let things slide. It would have been justified or upright to go to the right channel and report the incident. You are innocent and shouldn't be worried about the threats of an unlawful person." Eric smiled wryly and continued. "But in the world today, the right channels can no longer be trusted blindly, as almost everyone owes somebody else a favor, is in their pockets or want an extra slice of the pie."

Robert nodded. He could have stayed there and gone about

his business. He shouldn't have to lose anything, but he would know it was going on. He didn't want to associate with anyone that was mixed up in that mess. It was how he'd been raised.

"Heard you applied for other jobs? Had any luck?" Eric asked.

They'd gotten to the house which was just a mile from the golf course and were settling comfortably in front of a baseball game.

"No, not yet," It had been harder to get another job as quickly as he thought, considering the holiday season. But Robert was undeterred and didn't regret his decision once.

"Don't be discouraged. You made the right decision. Something will surely come up," Eric assured him.

Robert nodded before turning his attention back to the game. Things weren't turning out as planned but he was happy and thankful.

He was alive and in good health. He had a beautiful woman who loved him along with a wonderful encouraging family. Although he missed his parents, especially during the holidays, being together with Emma and her folks felt filled with life and joy. The holidays used to be hollow and empty.

***

Emma held her husband's hand and her mother's and waited for her father to finish saying grace.

The day had been hectic, with Emma assisting her mother in making large amounts of rice, vegetable sauce in curry, all the usual Thanksgiving fixings, and sandwiches.

Every Thanksgiving, Emma's mother always cooked a huge array of food and put them in takeout bags to hand out to the homeless shelters in downtown Chicago.

The tradition, which had been carried on for long enough that she'd forgotten when it started, was one of Emma's most beautiful childhood memories. She remembered what she'd asked her mother when she was ten while they walked into a shelter on a Thanksgiving morning.

"Mommy if God loved us all, why doesn't he give them houses like ours?"

Her mother smiled and tousled her hair. "Well child, with God, there is always the larger picture. We just have to trust him wholeheartedly."

Giving selflessly had its perks. It left her with a euphoric feeling at the joy and relief on faces. Looking around the table at her family, Emma was beyond thankful. Her parents were her best friends, mentors, and anytime she needed them, they were there. She was thankful for their love and support every single day.

She stole a covert glance at her husband who ladled gravy on his mashed potatoes. He looked relaxed and happy. Emma knew holidays were usually hard on him. She'd decided they start a new set of holiday traditions which he'd happily agreed to.

She was thrilled with the way he fit into her family. Her father loved him like a son and her mother was half in love with him herself. She called him a dreamy hunk when they weren't within earshot of her dramatic father.

"Emma, you should have seen me play today. You can ask Robert if I wasn't any good," Her father said suddenly after a forkful of salad. His eyes twinkled like a child's.

Robert laughed. "Yeah, he was good. Kinda surprising for a newbie."

Her father preened in the face of the compliment.

“I'd know if you were all that after you beat Norman. Then I'd believe you,” her mother said, snorting.

Eric shook his head, with an expression of mock hurt, and turned to Emma, “Em, darling, I hope you are more supportive of Robert than your mother is of me.”

Emma laughed and turned to look at Robert. He was already staring at her. Messages of warmth and love were received from his eyes as their gazes caught and held for a timeless gap. The muted sounds of clinking cutlery faded into oblivion, as did the room itself.

“They remind me of ourselves when we were younger, Eric.”

The sudden sound of her mother's wistful voice caused both Robert and Emma to break their connection as they became aware of their surroundings again.

Emma blushed and resumed eating while Robert just sat there, his eyes dreamy and hazy.

“We are thankful for the bounties on this table and the love which is palpable in this room. Ain't we, Maude?”

Emma's mother sighed. A contented smile hovering on her lips as she turned to her husband. “Yes, we are, Eric. There is so much to be thankful for.”

CHAPTER 9

Robert sat across from Jake Mortimer, his best friend and ex college roommate in the blue bistro on Main Street and stared at him with a mixture of incredulity and excitement.

If what he heard was correct, he could have the perfect surprise for Emma by Christmas.

"All you have to do is put in your place of employment and you are set. Lindsay and I are moving into our new home by Sunday," Jake said with pride and took a sip of his beer.

Jake worked with a construction crew and his wife Lindsay who was heavily pregnant and would be due any day so she had taken a break from the school where she taught. They'd been clamoring to get a new home, somewhere bigger with an extra room for the baby for months now and suddenly they had it.

Jake had called to meet up with him to tell him about the new mortgage bank which was giving loans for new homes in the suburbs where Robert and Emma drove through frequently to admire, the trim little houses on the row.

The houses were cheaper compared to the prices of apartments and houses in downtown Chicago. But Robert's excitement dimmed considerably when he heard Jake. He was yet to get a new job and the bank required a place of employment before they agreed to the loans.

Last night, when he and Emma had driven back home, a message had been waiting for him on the answering machine. It was from Wes, one of the ramp agents at Southwest Airlines. He told him of an opening at Delta Airline. They needed a ramper urgently and would be hiring immediately. Robert had quickly gone on their website and applied as Emma twirled around the room in excitement.

They'd promised him a response that morning, but it hadn't come in yet and it was midday already. Robert tried hard not to despair and took a huge gulp of his beer.

“How's the job search coming along?” Jake asked searching his face as if sensing the slight change of his mood.

Robert shrugged. “Slow, but I'm hopeful about something turning up soon.”

Jake nodded and made to say something else but thought better of it. He asked instead. “How is Em doing? It's been a long time since we saw you both at the garden.”

“She’s good. Work is busier at this time of year. We plan to take a drive there this weekend,” Robert answered with a smile.

Jake sighed. “Lindsay is so huge. She doesn't want to go anywhere till after the baby comes. We could have made it a group picnic.”

“Hey, congrats, man! How do you feel about it all?” Robert asked.

He and Emma had talked about starting a family soon after they were settled completely. He was both excited and worried at the same time.

“It's exciting and overwhelming in the beginning but when you feel your baby move for the first time. It's like magic. The feeling is indescribable, really,” Jake said with unrestrained emotion.

Robert clasped his friend's hand once more and thought of him and Emma someday with their own child. It was beyond thrilling.

***

The *Fix It by Emma* Christmas column Day One went remarkably well. Emma had dozens of letters to reply to and prepare for tomorrow's publication. The entire office was bustling with people rushing back and forth, trying to beat the deadline.

Emma looked up from an email she was reading and saw Rebecca and Marcus talking. Both wore heavy blushes on their faces which made Emma smile. That particular romance had gone faster than she thought.

Just this morning while she was speaking with Rebecca, she'd casually slipped Marcus into the conversation, praising his quick thinking and efficiency in saving her files. Rebecca had worn a telltale little smile all through and Emma had known she wasn't entirely immune to him. She hadn't done much there, the two had found themselves and with the heavy stares they were exchanging, something good was definitely brewing there.

It was almost lunchtime when Emma completed the article for the next publication and saved it on her new flash drive. She hadn't gotten time to grab breakfast and was quite hungry.

She stood and stretched. Grabbing her coat, she turned to leave for lunch. On second thought, she went back and retrieved her flash drive to slip into her coat pocket.

Outside was gray with the promises of snow. A gusty wind blew, and Emma tightened her coat around her body as she admired a newly decorated tree from the windows of Macy's.

The dresses hanging in the window were beautiful and classy. Emma stopped for a second to admire a long black strapless dinner gown with a lace trim. She wished her paycheck could be stretched enough to afford the dress for Christmas dinner.

"Hey, dreamer, why don't you go in and pick it up instead of just standing there drooling?”

Emma turned to see Susie Ann, dressed in jeans and a t-shirt, smiling devilishly at her with *Lift Me Up, Jesus* in red paint swipes. She seemed to have forgotten that she still wore her chef hat. Susie Ann was an assistant chef in a French restaurant in the Magnificent Miles plaza.

“Yeah, yeah, very funny, Susie. You think the hat goes with the T-shirt, don't you?” Emma teased. Susie Ann’s hand shot to her head, releasing a yelp and then a gasp as she yanked it off her head. Emma bent over laughing while her friend said, “I totally forgot, Em. You are such a dolt. Really? Thank heavens I love you.”

Emma linked arms together with her and they walked to their usual cafe for a strong cup of coffee and some grub.

They were halfway into lunch when Susie Ann's phone rang and she had to leave, complaining under her breath the whole time. Emma waved her off and took a huge bite out of her burger. Her phone rang almost immediately. She smiled when she saw the Caller ID but had to force her bite of burger down before answering it.

“Hi, baby,” Robert's voice came through the receiver like maple syrup on pancake.

“Hi, darling, how are you? How did breakfast go with Jake and how is Lindsay?” She asked all in one breath. Talking to Robert over the phone made her breathless and giddy like a child. His voice sounded warm and sexy.

“Lindsay is fine. She is due any day,” he replied.

“We should go visit them very soon, maybe after the picnic on Saturday.”

“That is perfect, Em. I have good news, and I just can't wait for you to get home to share.”

Emma's heart went into overdrive. This could only mean one thing. “You got the job, baby?”

Robert's excited yes came through like a warm blanket on a cold blizzard night. Emma squealed but toned down considerably as she turned to see some people in the lunch crowd staring at her.

“I'm taking you out to dinner tonight. Hurry home when you can, baby,” Robert said. He sounded incredibly relieved and happy.

“I can't wait to be home. See you soon,” Emma said and hung up after blowing him a kiss. She hurried through lunch, grinning from ear to ear, and returned to the office shortly after. She was more than ready to be done for the day, so she could go home to celebrate with her husband. It was still two weeks to Christmas, but the season's miracle was already drifting in the air.

Emma walked into the office on a cloud of excited bliss and was unaware of her surroundings until she almost got to her cubicle. Her joy petered out as the color went out of her face.

Caroline was frantically rifling through her desk drawer, jostling some papers in the process. Randall and Lauren, usually sitting on either side of her cubicle, were absent. She could only guess that they were still out on their lunch break.

Emma made a small sound of dismay as which drew Caroline's attention to her. She looked shell shocked and tried to put the papers back in and shut the drawer close.

“What are you doing, Caroline?” Emma asked quietly and walked closer to avoid drawing attention to them.

Caroline stood uncomfortably, her face etched with frustration as she looked everywhere but at Emma. “I was trying to find something I dropped on your desk a few days ago.”

“No, Caroline. We both know that isn't the truth. Please stop lying to me. I haven't done anything to hurt or jeopardize your job and I've done nothing remotely offensive to you. Why would you try to sabotage my job!" Emma hissed, her words exploding at the end.

A few heads turned towards their direction. Caroline burst into tears and made a beeline for the rest room.

Caroline wasn't the type to break down or burst into tears, even when she was in the wrong. Her anger temporarily forgotten; Emma followed her. She found Caroline wiping her eyes with a fold of toilet paper. She turned immediately when Emma entered. The place was deserted.

"I'm really sorry, Emma. I don't know what came over me. I was just blinded with jealousy at your easy nature and how everyone likes you and..." She broke off suddenly and looked away from Emma. "I will go to the management and confess to everything. I really can't believe how low I've sunk. I may have some issues, but this bitter person is not who I am."

Emma heard the despair in her voice and felt sorry for her. "Caroline, I won't say anything. You know what would happen if Lydia found out. This will stay between us only if you promise me something."

"Anything, Emma," Caroline said, her eyes imploring as she looked up at Emma.

Emma closed the gap between them and held her hand. "Would you tell me what is really wrong after work? Maybe a quick drink at the lounge next door?"

Caroline contemplated for a few seconds before nodding. "I'm really sorry, Emma," She whispered before slipping out of the restroom.

Emma had mixed feelings. She'd always admired Caroline's journalistic abilities and respected her greatly despite what every other person in the press thought of her. She never suspected Caroline was jealous of her.

Slowly rising to the editing department, Caroline was extremely good with manipulating words and evoking a reader's interest with the twists of her articles.

The twist of the doorknob jolted Emma out of her reverie. She gave a quick smile to the intern who entered the restroom before Emma left with a million thoughts rolling around in her head.

***

Emma got home late for dinner. She'd called Robert earlier promising to bring their favorite Thai takeout on her way back.

Her one drink with Caroline had turned into an evening of revelations and tears. Emma was subdued as she entered the apartment.

Robert pulled her in for a hug. Afterward, she gave him the bags of takeout.

"You don't look so good, Em. Long day?" He asked, peering into her face.

Emma sighed as she shrugged off her coat and followed Robert into the kitchen.

"I'm sorry we couldn't go to dinner. Something incredible came up at the office."

Robert raised a brow. "Really? Then why are you wearing that frown like you lost a best friend?"

"Oh, Robert, I just want you to hold me," Emma replied and went into her husband's open arms.

Robert bent to pick her up and then carried her to the couch where he sat with her. He cuddled with her as he ran a soothing hand down her hair.

Emma told him everything about finding Caroline at her desk and the drink afterwards. She marveled at how a person looked perfect and put together but nursed a huge grief inside.

Caroline's husband whom she'd been married to for almost seven years was an unrepentant cheat who paraded his affairs before her face. She had tried to get them in counseling so many times, but it never worked. She loved him so much and couldn't bear to divorce him. That had been taken from her when he moved out of the house two weeks ago and sent her divorce papers. She'd confessed to Emma about trying to keep it together and pleaded with him to reconsider but it had been a moot point.

They'd both lost a child years ago, and Caroline had been more attached to him after that. The divorce would take away the only lifeline she had to the child they'd lost.

Emma's eyes grew moist. She'd held the other woman's hand while she let out all the tears she'd been holding in.

Robert cuddled with Emma till she felt slightly better. They reheated dinner an hour later and ate in silence, each deep in thought.

Emma sent a prayer heavenward for the gift of her husband's love. Even though things weren't exactly perfect with them, they loved each other deeply and that was enough.

CHAPTER 10

The second week in December flew by like migrating birds in a hurry to get to warmth before winter came. Emma had been incredibly busy with work and rarely saw her husband except late at night.

Robert's new job was tasking as Christmas drew closer. The airport was crowded with travelers and the airlines were incredibly busy. Delta Airlines weren't as large as Southwest, but the season brought in a huge influx of travelers that kept them overbooked.

Robert left early in the morning and returned really late at night to grab a quick dinner before bed. Sometimes he was too tired to eat and fell straight into bed after taking a bath.

They hadn't talked about decorating the apartment for Christmas or the presents they were getting for each other. Usually, they gave each other a budget of fifty to hundred dollars for gifts. Depending on how well they were doing and made it a point to purchase all their gifts with that challenge. They loved it because it made them find creative and unique ways to purchase gifts for each other and it meant more to them than just going to the store and pulling a few random gifts to the cart.

Emma texted Robert as she got off work that Friday. She knew he wouldn't make it in time for dinner but wanted his input in the decorations and to know if they were going to continue their tradition of budget gifts.

She planned to spend the evening teaching Ingrid the methods of making her mother's pecan pie. Ida was away visiting some cousins and Emma couldn't put it off any longer. She avoided walking down the Avenue because of the distracting window displays and treated herself to an Uber ride.

She had Saturday off to go shopping for decorations and gifts for everyone. Emma was filled with boundless excitement over that prospect.

Shopping, especially shopping for Christmas left her with an excitement that she couldn't describe. She didn't understand the trepidation and anxiety her friends encountered when shopping for Christmas. It filled her with such delight and the only issues Emma usually encountered, was having to pick one gift in the vast array of offerings in the mall.

***

Robert read Emma's message with a smile at the corner of his lips. He replied after a while, letting her know she could decorate all she wanted. About the gift, they would continue their tradition as they usually did, hopefully things would get better over time. He refrained from telling her about his surprise even if it was practically bursting from the seams to be spilled.

He had more news to share when he got home later which he knew would leave Emma very upset. The Airline was sending him off to La Guardia in the morning, and he was expected to be there for nine whole days before Christmas.

A huge storm was headed toward New York in the next couple of days, and they needed all the help they could get to move passengers out of the airport before its possible shut down.

He knew Emma wouldn't take kindly to him being absent for nine days. He mentally prepared for the separation as he went back to work, eager to get home and overcome his own particular private storm.

***

Emma handed Robert a cup of cocoa and went behind to massage his shoulders. He had been stressing so hard lately and the results were a stiff neck and taut shoulders.

The evening had gone remarkably well, with Ingrid not only managing to not burn the entire complex down but making the perfect pecan pie that astounded and amazed them both. She'd insisted on taking pictures of it and begged Emma to send it on Facebook to Ida's new account. She wasn't big on the internet but Ida, with all her reserve, spent all day on it.

"So, any idea of what gift you want this year?" Emma asked, breaking the companionable silence.

"No, you know my preferences, baby. Anything you buy for me will be a great gift," Robert answered and turned to give her a kiss. "How about you? Any special thing on your wish list?"

"You always manage to find me great, incredibly amazing presents, Robbie, so I have nothing in mind at the moment." Emma was telling him the absolute truth.

Compared to her, Robert spent more time trying to find the best gifts and, most of the time, they weren't even on her radar for holiday shopping. He bought the quirkiest, most surprising gifts of the both of them.

She cuddled up in his arms and turned on the television. Her favorite movie, *It's a Wonderful Life,* was playing.

She snuggled deeper into his arm but turned a minute later to see Robert regarding her with an uncomfortable expression on his face.

"Hey, baby, anything wrong?"

He grimaced and pulled her closer. "I have something to tell you, love. They are sending me over to La Guardia tomorrow afternoon, and I will be there until the twenty second. Apparently a huge storm is hitting New York tomorrow. They're pulling in help to clear passengers out before they shut down parts of the airport. All this with additional pay of course." He added hastily at the widening of her eyes.

"Shut down! It's two days until Christmas and you'll be gone for almost a week. Can't they find others closer to New York?"

Emma was upset, this wasn't how she envisioned her first Christmas as a newlywed. They were supposed to decorate the apartment together and attend some events before Christmas Eve.

"I know, I'm sorry. There's nothing I can do about it. Not to worry, I'll be back before Christmas and we can also use the extra money. I'll bring home the Christmas tree in the morning before I leave. I'm sorry, Emma. You know this is a new job, and I also checked the box that said I was willing to go where they needed me in case of emergency or weather situations."

"Yeah well, okay," Emma answered after a while. She couldn't hide the disappointment in her voice.

"Come here, baby. I will make it up to you, believe me, love. When I get a few days off after Christmas, we can do anything we want to make up for the time I'll spend away," Robert implored, opening his arms to her.

Emma went to him grudgingly after some seconds. "I understand, but it doesn't mean I have to like it."

"I know, baby, I know," Robert answered and bent to kiss her hair.

The next afternoon, Emma stood on tiptoe to kiss Robert goodbye before he left. She inhaled the scent of pine and brushed her hand over the sticky pins of the fresh Christmas tree Robert had bought at the farmer's market in Wilmette.

She hurried to dress to go downtown to shop for decorations and gifts. Emma planned to make the most of the time Robert was away and made sure he returned to a completely different apartment. She would focus on work and hang out with Lynn on the weekend and hope the time flew fast so Robert could get back home in time for Christmas.

The next few days flew past in a blur. Emma had decorated the apartment with Christmas lights and garland. She bought sprigs of mistletoe and hung it over every door in the apartment and shiny ornaments for the tree.

She'd also gotten presents for her parents and friends and a beautiful engraved watch for Robert which was slightly over the initial budget, but she didn't mind one bit. He was going to love it.

The TV had been tuned to the weather channel for days now. The blizzard had dumped record snowfall over New England but managed to bypass much of New York. A new storm was expected within the next few days, but Emma wasn't worried. Robert would be home between storms, and they'd be able to have their first Christmas together.

CHAPTER 11

Emma had just finished making herself a sandwich on the evening of the twentieth when her phone rang from the living room. She hurried to get it and couldn't stop her excitement when she saw it was Robert.

"Hey, love! Just a couple more days until you're home," she said before he could get anything out.

"Well, that's why I'm calling you. This new storm is moving in faster than expected and, if it hits La Guardia, I won't be able to get out of the city."

"What?! I thought you said you were leaving on the twenty second, that's only two days away!" Emma was angry and trying not to take it out on Robert. Mother Nature was determined to make the holiday difficult for her and she wasn't pleased with any of it.

"I know. Apparently, the storm is coming in faster than they thought, so there's not much I can do besides wait it out. I'll try to do what I can, but I can't make any promises," Robert told her. He was disappointed too. He yearned to spend their first Christmas together and never anticipated being stuck in an airport on such an important Christmas.

"I'm sorry, love. I'll do everything in my power to get home for Christmas."

After they said their goodbyes, Emma got teary-eyed as she hung up the phone.

All she wanted for Christmas was for Robert to be home and it looked like it wasn't going to happen. She calmed down after a while and called her mom to explain the situation.

Her mom, sympathetic as always, told her not to worry and to come over on Christmas Eve if Robert wasn't home by then. They would try to make the holiday special and then celebrate again when he got back to Chicago.

The twenty second came and went, and then it was the twenty third and twenty fourth. Each day, Robert called to tell her that the flights were grounded, and no one was leaving La Guardia. She knew it was hopeless to think her husband would be home in time to celebrate Christmas, and that the beautiful gift she wanted to give him would have to wait a few more days. She lay in bed for a long while, refusing to stand and get on with the day.

The snow had started to fall gently and it looked like it was going to be a perfect white Christmas, but Emma was in no mood to celebrate. After lying there for an hour, the phone rang and jostled her awake as she began to doze off.

For a moment, she thought it was Robert telling her he'd found a flight home, but her screen flashed the word 'Mom'. Emma tried not to let her disappointment show.

"Hey, Mom. Looks like I'll be coming over tonight. Robert still hasn't gotten out of the airport."

Her mom tried to cheer her up. "Okay, well there's nothing we can do, so we will just have to celebrate as soon as he gets home. Come over for dinner. I'm making roast beef and mashed potatoes—your favorite."

Emma felt bad for acting like a baby, but she was grateful her mom was going to the extra trouble to make her feel better.

"Thanks, Mom. I'll be over in a little while. Dinner sounds amazing." They said goodbye and she hung up the phone before lounging a while longer on the bed.

As she sat there staring out the window looking at the beautiful snowfall, Emma was upset at herself. Robert was the one sitting in an airport without any friends and family on Christmas Eve and she was the one throwing the pity party.

She was embarrassed for acting so selfish and decided to call Robert to apologize and tell him she loved him. Emma called his phone and was surprised to have it go straight to voicemail, so she tried again.

When the line didn't go through, she sent him a text message telling him she was sorry, and they would celebrate as soon as he got back to the city. She figured he had no reception, or his phone was dead since there were probably a limited number of outlets to use in an airport full of stranded passengers.

She stepped into the shower and got ready to go to her parent's house.

Inside her parents' house was reminiscent of Emma's childhood. The scent of warm roast permeated the air while the Christmas tree was full of tinsel and sat glistening in a corner. She loved Christmas at her parents' house and was sad that Robert wasn't there to enjoy it.

Her mom came out of the kitchen, her apron dusted with flour after baking for the afternoon and gave Emma a hug. She tried to make everything as nice as possible to get her mind off it.

Emma followed her mom into the kitchen to help make the mashed potatoes, her favorite side dish with roast beef. They made small talk and kept busy in their own section of the kitchen.

When dinner was ready, Emma began to set the table.

"Dear, set an extra space. One of your father's friend is joining us for dinner tonight because we didn't want him to feel lonely," her mom said as Emma grabbed a handful of forks. Emma did as she was told, setting the extra knife and fork in the space across from where she would sit. They placed the roast beef, mashed potatoes and vegetables in different serving dishes and set them on the table.

"Mom, when is Dad's friend going to get here? I'm starving," Emma asked.

"He should be here soon. He mentioned around seven." Her mom replied.

Since it was five minutes until seven, Emma was relieved she didn't have to wait much longer to dig into her mother's wonderful meal. The minutes ticked by as slow as possible, until it was almost five after seven. Emma was getting impatient and ask her mother again where Dad's friend was when someone rang the doorbell.

Finally! Now we can eat. Emma thought. She sat on the couch, waiting for her mom or dad to come answer the door.

From the kitchen, she heard her mom yell out, "Emma, answer the door. Will you?"

When she opened it, Emma almost had a heart attack. Robert was smiling and holding a bouquet of flowers. Emma squealed and threw her arms around his neck, hugging him hard and squishing the flowers in the process.

After holding onto him for a minute, she stepped back and ha to ask, "I can't believe it! How did you get here, I thought you said the flights were grounded?"

"Someone told me to take a train to Philadelphia and hop on a flight there, since the storm didn't hit that area of the coast. I told your mom to keep it a surprise!" Robert answered with a wink.

Her mom was standing behind them with a mischievous smile, happy she pulled everything off perfectly.

"Mom! How could you keep that secret from me?" Emma lovingly chided her mom.

Emma was so happy to have her husband home for their first Christmas that she forgot about the engraved watch until the clock struck midnight.

For almost a week or two, Emma had been planning to spend the perfect Christmas with her husband and had resigned herself to the fact that their perfect Christmas wouldn't come to pass but Robert had surprised and given her the best gift of all by returning in time to spend Christmas with her.

***

Robert rested his head on his wife's head and sighed contentedly. He couldn't imagine having to spend the first Christmas married to Emma away from home.

He felt the wetness of her tears on his chest and raised her face gently to meet his. “Baby, I'm home. You should stop crying now. I'm beginning to feel like I've done something wrong.”

“I'm sorry.” She said with a sniff. “I really thought you wouldn't make it back home and I was so sad we wouldn't be together for Christmas.”

“Me too, baby. I'm so glad to be back home with you,” Robert replied.

They had driven back home from Emma's parent's house at midnight and were wrapped in each other's arms, snuggled under the covers.

“I've still not giving you my present and you didn't even ask,” Robert said, patting her lustrous brown hair.

Emma looked up at him and beamed. “Being back home is the best present ever. What more can I ask for?”

Robert grinned. “But I have a present for you, darling, and we would have to dress up and take a drive for it.”

Emma bounded up in excitement. “Really! Tell me what it is,” She pleaded, bouncing on the mattress in childish delight.

“It's meant to be a surprise. Come on, go dressed,” Robert said and got off the bed.

“You are full of surprises, Mr. McAllister. I don't know if I can take anymore.” Emma said with twinkling eyes and finally left the bed to put on something warm for the drive.

Robert led a blindfolded Emma to the front porch of their new home. He'd driven there before coming to her parent's last night to hang the sign which read 'Welcome Home' in the front of the freshly painted door.

“Get this off me, Robert. I am dying to see what the surprise is,” Emma said impatiently and groped around for his hand.

“Anyone ever told you how impatient you are?” He teased, tickling her nose.

“Yes, you do almost every day. Now take this off me, baby.”

Robert laughed at her comment and fetched the key of the house from his back pocket.

He'd kept communications with Jake about getting the house ready for Christmas morning and was impressed with the way it looked.

Reaching behind, he pulled off the blindfold from Emma's face and watched as she blinked several times before staring at the sign on the door.

“I don't understand, Robert. Where is this…”

“Welcome home, Emma,” Robert said with a smile, cutting her off and dangled the keys in front of her. “Welcome to our new home, baby.”

Emma stood there transfixed. She looked from the door to him and back to the door. “How did you... I don't understand Robert, how did you do this?” She asked in a whisper, tears springing to her eyes.

“Merry Christmas, baby... It's the season of miracles.” Robert answered, a warm smile on his face as he gazed lovingly into Emma's eyes.

“Oh, Robert, I love you!” Was all she said before losing herself in his embrace.

It was indeed the season of miracles....

Book Sample

Sara in Montana, ASIN: B00GU2DJBO

Chapter 1

Sara pulled up in front of the small drug store and leaned her forehead against the steering wheel for a brief moment. She was somewhere in eastern Montana, not sure exactly where, but she had been driving for two days straight. She had seen the sign for the little town and pulled off the highway in desperation. She was hoping to find a place to hole up, for just one night.

Exhausted, she pushed herself back from the steering wheel, reached across the console for her purse and turned to open the door. The harsh winter wind rushed into the car as she pushed the door open. Shivering, she pulled her thin shirt around herself and carefully navigated the snow and ice until she reached the sidewalk. Thank goodness, someone had shoveled the surface. Her thin tennis shoes were no match for the snow and she could already feel the moisture seeping through.

Pulling the door open, she hurried inside and then paused. On any other day, she would have stopped to appreciate the Norman Rockwell-like scene before her. The sounds of Christmas music filled the air and the old-fashioned soda fountain was decorated with garlands and tiny Christmas lights. A tinsel Christmas tree stood atop the countertop and fake snow had been sprayed around the mirror which made up the bar's back wall. Black and white tiles and red vinyl booths completed the picture.

Christmas was still several weeks away but the festive atmosphere in the store just augmented Sara's situation. She should be baking cookies with her niece and fighting the crowds at the mall. Instead, she was in the middle of nowhere and running out of options.

Right now, her only goal was finding a restroom.

As she scanned the back of the store, looking for a sign that would direct her to their bathroom facilities, she was once again wracked by a coughing spell that had her holding her ribs and bending over at the waist in an attempt to control the pain. She had begun coughing yesterday morning, and the coughing fits had gotten so bad she had been forced to stop driving several times during the day.

Managing to get control of her breathing once again, she straightened and started to move forward, only to run into a wall of muscle. Quickly glancing up, she moved back as she looked into the bluest eyes she had ever seen.

"I'm sorry," she told the man in front of her, hoarsely. Swallowing, she tried to find her voice again, "I didn't see you there. Excuse me." Sara attempted to walk around the man only to find her path blocked as he moved with her.

"That cough sounds pretty nasty. Are you okay?" Trent Harding asked. He had been sitting at the counter talking to Jeb Matthews, the drugstore owner, when he had seen the strange vehicle pull up in front of the store.

As the town sheriff, Trent knew every vehicle the 1,356 residents of Castle Peaks, Montana drove. The silver Camry parked out front was not one of them.

"I'm fine," Sara replied, as she looked at her feet. Not quite meeting his eyes, she asked, "Um, is there a bathroom here I could use?" Thanks to her latest coughing fit, finding a bathroom was becoming her number one priority.

"Sure. Just go straight back. It's on your left," Trent gestured behind him.

Sara cut her eyes back to his briefly and just nodded. Edging around him, she quickly navigated her way through the aisles, finding the bathroom and closing herself inside.

Trent watched the small woman until she located the bathroom. His radar was on high alert as he took in her appearance. Wearing a thin button down shirt over a t-shirt, well-worn jeans, and tennis shoes that appeared to be wet from their encounter with the snow, she was completely under-dressed for a Montana winter.

Puzzled that someone would venture out into the weather like that, especially while they were sick, Trent turned back to look at the vehicle parked out front. The license plates showed the vehicle was registered in California. Making a mental note of the plate number, he turned and took his seat at the bar again.

"That little gal seems like she's not feeling so well. That's a pretty bad sounding cough," Jeb said, as he finished wiping down the counter.

"Yeah. Car's registered in California."

"California? She's a long way from home then."

Trent and Jeb both turned at the sound of the bathroom door opening and watched as the young woman headed back towards the front of the store. As she drew closer, Trent got a better look at her and could not help but smile in approval. She was only around 5' 6" tall, almost a foot shorter than his 6' 4" height, with gorgeous baby blue eyes framed by long lashes. Her complexion was blemished by the weather and her long blonde hair was pulled up into a haphazard ponytail that was slightly askew. Her clothing did nothing to hide the curves hidden underneath.

Coming around from behind the counter, Jeb wiped his hands on the towel at his waist and held his hand out as she approached him, "Good afternoon, Jeb Matthews at your service. What can I help you with?"

Sara hesitantly shook the older gentleman's hand. He reminded her of her late Uncle Thomas. His white hair and friendly demeanor helped to put Sara at ease. Swallowing, Sara said, "Would you happen to have any cough medicine?" Coughing again, she held onto her ribs until the fit had passed. She felt light headed as the spell eased, and struggled to catch her breath.

Jeb watched the young woman start coughing again and hurried around the counter, returning with a bottle of water which he uncapped and pushed into her hands. "Drink some of this and see if it helps."

Sara took the water and drank several small sips before she felt able to talk once again. "Thank you."

"Let me show you where I keep the cold remedies and we'll see if there's something there that might help you with that cough." Jeb indicated that she should follow him with a nod of his head.

After looking at several shelves, he bent and retrieved several boxes of cough syrup. Handing them to Sara, "One of these should do the trick. Have you been running a fever?"

Sara took the boxes he held out to her, and pretending to look at the usage directions, she shrugged one shoulder, "I don't really know. Probably…I…um…" Sara handed the boxes back and once again wrapped her arms around herself. She needed her glasses. Without them, she could barely make out the large printed brand name, let alone read the smaller typed directions for how to use the medicine. They were in the car but she did not have the energy to go get them. It was only cough syrup. They were all alike, weren't they? Sara didn't really know. She couldn't ever remember being this sick. "Maybe you could just choose one for me?"

Something was off here, but Jeb couldn't quite figure out what. Chalking it up to her not feeling well, he turned to where Trent sat observing their interaction, "Hey, Trent, which one of these would you recommend for her cough?" Jeb held both boxes aloft so Trent could see them.

Trent stood up and walked over to look at the boxes himself. Sara glanced at him quickly and then looked away again. He was wearing a badge. How had she missed that the first time? That was the last thing she needed right now. She wasn't sure how far David Patterson's influence reached, but if he had California law enforcement on his side, God only knew whom else he could influence.

Reaching out and removing the first box of cough syrup from Jeb's hand, she told him, "I'm sure this one will be fine. If you could ring me up I'll be on my way."

Sara turned and started to head towards the checkout counter, only to find her way once again blocked by a wall of muscle. Looking up she found her gaze trapped in that of the sheriff. He was the most handsome man she had ever seen. Luxurious hair that just begged to have her fingers running through it framed a strong face. Eyes that made her think of the night sky and a mouth that made her stomach flip filled her vision. Glancing down, the vision only got better. His shirt did nothing to hide the sculpted muscles of his chest and arms. Blushing at where her eyes had been headed, she forced her eyes to discontinue their southern perusal. She raised her eyes back up to see him giving her the same visual inspection.

She was gorgeous. Trent watched as her eyes scanned his face and then traveled down his body. He quickly did his own appraisal and definitely liked what he saw. Glancing down at her ring finger, he was pleased to see it vacant. He wasn't sure whom she was in town to visit, but he hoped she would stick around long enough for him to get to know her a little better.

"Excuse me," Sara attempted to go around the sheriff again.

Again, he moved with her, stopping her forward motion. "My

name's Trent Harding, and you are?" Trent held his hand out, and when she didn't seem inclined to take it, he slowly reached up and rubbed his forehead, considering her skittishness all the while.

"Just passing through." Sara didn't have it in her to stand and trade niceties with this man. He was definitely someone she would have enjoyed looking at in another life, but now she needed to pay for the cough syrup and find the highway again. There were still several hours until dark and she needed to find some place to hunker down for the night. She should probably fill up with gas before leaving so that she could keep the heater going throughout the night.

For the last several nights, Sara had found secluded rest spots and spent her nights sleeping for short periods before the cold would force her to start the car and run the heater. She hoped that one more night and another day of driving would place her far enough away from San Francisco that she could stop and finally get some much needed rest. She was more tired than she could ever remember being and the coughing spells took every ounce of spare energy she could muster. What she wouldn't give to curl up in a nice warm bed and sleep for the next 48 hours.

Trent's radar went on alert even more as she attempted to get around him again. Taking hold of her elbow, he felt her stiffen, but she didn't try to pull away. He turned her toward the register and together they walked towards it. Looking down at her, he tried again, "I still didn't catch your name."

Sara looked up at Trent, and licking her lips replied, "I'm Sara." Trent watched her tongue come out and wet her dry lips, then felt his body instantly respond. What was it about this woman? He'd never felt this instant attraction before.

"It's nice to meet you, Sara. I see your car is registered in California. That's quite a ways from here. Are you visiting family for the holidays up here?"

Sara shook her head, "No."

Jeb took the cough syrup from her and rang it up. "That'll be $10.83."

Sara swallowed and forced her sense of dread down. She had been very careful only to use cash since she started running, but that was mostly gone now. Seeing no other way to get what she needed, she asked, "Do you accept credit cards?"

"Sure we do." Sara handed her card over and then signed for the purchase. Now she really needed to get on the road again. She had no doubt in her mind that David and his goons would be monitoring her credit cards. Within hours they would know exactly where she was. Grabbing the bag that Jeb handed her, she turned and hurried towards the front door, coughing as she went.

Seeing her hurried attempt to leave the store, Jeb called after her, "Miss, don't you want your receipt?" When she didn't turn or respond, Jeb slowly put the receipt in the cash register drawer and watched her exit his store. Concern etched across his face. That little gal was sick and needed someone to look after her. With a raised eyebrow, he gave Trent a look and nodded his head towards the door.

Trent watched Sara stop on the sidewalk and double over when the coughing fit didn't immediately subside. That was one sick woman who had no business driving around right now. Deciding it was his civic duty to try and talk some sense into her, he went after her. As he stepped outside, he wished he had grabbed his jacket. A winter storm was headed their way, and the wind had been picking up all day long.

Sara hurt so badly she didn't know how she was going to be able to continue driving anymore. Taking shallow breaths to try and quell the most recent coughing spell, and shivering from the biting winds, she started towards the vehicle only to find her path blocked once again. What was it with this man? She didn't have the energy to deal with this right now.

“Ma’am, I really think you need to think about getting off the road for the night. You don’t seem like you’re in the best shape for driving on the highway.”

Sara shook her head. She needed to leave town - now. “Sheriff, thanks for your concern, but I really need to be on my way.”

“Where are you headed?” Something wasn’t adding up and he could see Sara growing more agitated by the minute.

“I…I just need to get back on the highway. I’m running kinda late because I haven’t been feeling well.” Wrapping her arms around herself, she tried to shield herself from the ever-increasing wind and cold.

“Running late?” Trent could see her start to shiver, but was more interested in getting some answers. He was a good reader of people, and this little gal was definitely hiding something.

Sara nodded quickly, trying to think of something that would reassure the Sheriff and get him to leave her alone. Where was she again? Oh yeah, Montana. What did she know about Montana…Helena was the capital. Striving to keep her voice even and not give way to the lie she was about to tell, she looked Trent in the eyes as she told him, “I’m headed to Helena. My fiancé is flying in tomorrow and I’m supposed to pick him up at the airport so we can spend the holidays with his parents.” Sara barely hid her nerves as she spun the tale.

“Helena, huh? You’ve still got several hours of driving left ahead of you. And there’s another snowstorm supposed to start later this evening.”

“That’s okay. I’ve driven in the snow before. I’ll be fine, but I would like to get back on the road.” Sara’s voice was only a whisper by this time. Her throat felt as if it was on fire, her head was throbbing, and her chest hurt if she tried to take a deep breath. Combine that with the biting wind and uncontrollable shivers that had taken over her body, and she knew her ability to continue on her journey was in danger of coming to an abrupt halt.

"Well, if you are sure." Trent moved a step back and opened the car door for her. Surreptitiously glancing inside the backseat, he saw a small duffel bag, along with several blankets and a pillow. It almost appeared as if she had been sleeping in her car.

Sara nodded and slid into the driver's seat. The cold wind had her teeth chattering and her hands were so cold, she wasn't sure if she could turn the key in the ignition. After fumbling to grasp the key for several moments, she finally caught hold of it and started the car. Turning towards the open door and the waiting Sheriff, she gave him a small smile and said, "Thank you for your help."

Trent returned her smile. "No problem. You drive safe now. Merry Christmas."

Sara was so cold; all she could do was give a slight nod in recognition of his well wishes. She did not have the energy to dwell on the upcoming holiday season and what might have been. Right now, her survival was the only thing she could focus on and that required her to keep pushing farther east.

Trent stepped back, closing her car door and watched as she put the car into gear and headed back towards the highway.

Try as she might, the sheriff's parting words stayed with Sara as she backed out and headed the car back towards the highway. It was supposed to have been a wonderful Christmas. She had looked forward to her first holiday season as a married woman, decorating a tree together for the first time with her husband, inviting their family and friends over for dinner. She mentally gave herself a shake. Those dreams were gone now. Any Christmas spirit she did have vanished along with her hopes and dreams of being happily married to the man of her dreams. Nightmares are what they had become.

Wanting to take her mind off her morose thoughts, she turned the radio back on and tried not to think about what might have been. The radio announcer had just finished his weather report and it wasn't sounding promising for her. They were expecting up to a foot of snow, and a travel advisory had just been issued for central Montana as the winds were supposed to kick up and blow snow across the highway known to be treacherous. Sara had never driven in the snow prior to this trip and had scared herself several times during early morning hours as her car skidded on the icy patches dotting the highway.

Sarah briefly thought about turning around and seeing if the small town had any type of hotel accommodations, but then she remembered having used her credit card to pay for the cough syrup. Anyone looking for her would be able to track her credit card use. She definitely needed to put some miles between herself and Castle Peaks, Montana. Another state or two between them would suit her just fine.

****

Rubbing his hands together, Trent quickly re-entered the drugstore, seeing Jeb standing at the front window watching her car drive away.

"You couldn't convince her to stay, huh?"

"No. She says she's headed to Helena to pick her fiancé up from the airport in the morning. I hope she beats the storm. I don't think that little car of hers was meant to handle a Montana blizzard."

"She doesn't look like she's ready for a Montana winter. That girl didn't even have a coat on."

Trent's radar was still going off. Something here just wasn't right. "Hey Jeb, let me see that credit card receipt she signed."

Jeb looked at Trent, wondering what was going through his head, but opened the drawer and took out the receipt. Glancing at her signature, he read, "Sara Brownell."

Trent took the offered receipt and a notepad from his pocket. Jotting down her license plate number, he added her name and then pocketed the pad and the pen. "I'm gonna go back over to the office and check a couple of things out real quick. I'll see you later on."

"You gonna run that girl through the system?" Jeb asked.

"I'm gonna go run the plates first. Make sure the vehicle's registered to her and that everything's in order."

Jeb nodded and said, "I hope you don't find that girl's in any trouble. I get the sense that she's had it pretty rough recently."

Trent didn't reply. He would reserve his comments until after he had some facts. His gut told him that she was in trouble; what sort, he aimed to find out.

Chapter 2

Sara had almost made it back to the highway when another coughing fit struck. This one was the worst yet and she had no choice but to pull off the side of the road and place her car into park. Holding her chest, she tried desperately to stop the coughing. Knowing there was no one around to see, she gave free rein to the tears that came with the agonizing pain. As the coughing fit stopped, she pushed the driver's seat back a little and pulled her knees up to her chest, trying to hold herself together.

Sara leaned her head back and closed her eyes, trying to take slow, calm breaths so it didn't hurt as badly. Finally able to breathe easier, she opened the bottle of cough syrup and took several small sips. Washing it down with the rest of the bottled water the storeowner had given her, she closed her eyes again and waited for the medicine to begin to work.

"God, I don't know if you're there, or if you even care, but I need a miracle. I know it's the Christmas season and all, but I'm scared and I don't know what to do anymore." Taking a deep breath, Sara tried to clear her mind and push back the panic that had been prominent for the last several days.

She was in Montana, not California, and David Patterson was nowhere around. She would be successful in finding a place to hide. She just needed to get back on the highway. Opening her eyes, she started to sit up; only to sink back down again as the urge to cough made itself known. Maybe another few minutes wouldn't hurt. She would just sit here and take a small rest. Turning the ignition off, she grabbed a blanket from the backseat and wrapped it around her to keep warm. Leaning her head back against the seat, she allowed her eyes to close as she concentrated on keeping her breathing slow and even.

***

Trent fixed himself a cup of coffee as he waited for the license plate information to appear on his computer. He was hoping to find nothing, but his gut told him that would probably not be the case.

Seeing the message indicator start flashing, he returned to his desk and took a sip of his coffee before clicking the screen open. As the information came up on the screen, he sat up straight and cursed. The car was registered to one David Patterson, who had been attacked two days prior and his car reported stolen. His new bride, Sara Brownell, was wanted for questioning in the attack and theft.

That little gal had attacked a full grown man and stolen his car? Again, his radar was going off. He quickly ran another search on Sara Brownell and wasn't surprised to find that she was squeaky clean. Not even a parking ticket was tied to her name.

On a hunch, he ran her groom's name through the same database. Checking the time, he saw that less than 15 minutes had passed since she had pulled away from the drugstore. She couldn't have gotten far. He wasn't quite sure what was going on, but something in his gut told him it was imperative that he find her and bring her back to town. She needed help and he was the only one in a position to help her at this point.

As the search came back for David Patterson, his fears were confirmed. It wasn't that he had a long record, or even any arrests, but the yellow flag on the account identified him as a person of interest with the feds and that meant there was more to this situation than at first appeared.

Grabbing his coat and hat, he sprinted for the jeep parked out front and headed towards the highway. He didn't even take time to tell Becky, his secretary, goodbye. Sara was in trouble and although he couldn't sanction her having stolen a car, he wanted to be the one to bring her in and see if he could help her in any way. She didn't seem like a criminal to him, but it was his duty to enforce the law. He would find her, and then make a few phone calls and see what other information he could obtain on her groom.

As he neared the entrance to the highway, he spotted her vehicle pulled off to the side of the road. Slowing down, he parked behind the vehicle and noticed that it wasn't running. Cursing again, he climbed out of the jeep and approached the driver's side door. The windows had become fogged up, but he could see her huddled underneath one of the blankets on the front seat.

Not wanting to startle her, but needing to get her attention, he called her name several times, but she didn't seem to hear him. When tapping on the window didn't get her attention either, he tried the door, finding it unlocked. Didn't she have any sense of self-preservation? He definitely needed to have a conversation with her about safety.

Opening the car door, he noticed the car was still warm inside, but Sara didn't stir. Reaching inside, he placed his hand on her head, and then on her neck, looking for a pulse. Her forehead was clammy and even though she was shivering, she was sweating profusely. Her pulse was strong, but as another cough wracked her body, he could see that she was unconscious. Whether by exhaustion or illness, Sara Brownell was a danger to herself as well as others as long as she remained behind the wheel of a car.

Carefully lifting her into his arms, he tucked the blanket around her, carried her to his jeep, and buckled her into the passenger seat. Returning to her vehicle, he grabbed her purse and the small duffel bag from the back seat and then turned on the car's emergency flashers. Sprinting back to the driver's side, he jumped in and headed back to town. Getting on the radio, he contacted Becky, "Get in touch with Dr. Baker and tell him I'm bringing over a young woman. She's been coughing for several days and appears to be running a fever. She's passed out cold. Tell him I'll be at his clinic in 15 minutes."

"Will do. Is there anything else I can do?"

"Yeah, will you get a hold of Jim over at the filling station and have him come tow her car back to town. It's pulled off the road about a mile from the highway entrance. Silver Camry with California plates. I turned the flashers on and the key is under the floor mat."

"I've got it. Where do you want him to tow it?"

"Have him park it over at his place for now. I'll call him later and give him further instructions."

"Okay. Good luck."

Trent looked over at his passenger, still passed out cold and a wave of tenderness passed over him. He didn't know what it was about this woman, but he felt a need to protect her. Seeing her start to stir, he reached over and placed a hand on her shoulder. "Sara, can you hear me?"

Sara felt warmth and for the first time in days, she didn't feel the urge to cough as she took in a slow, deep breath. Her ribs still felt tender, but the agonizing pain was gone. Slowly opening her eyes, she saw that she was in a moving vehicle and immediately tried to sit up as panic assailed her.

"Shush, you're okay. Just sit back and relax. I'm taking you to see Dr. Baker and then we'll get everything else sorted out."

Turning her head to locate the source of the voice, she found herself sinking in the warm gaze of the sheriff, Trent Harding. "Where…" Swallowing, she tried again, "Where am I?"

"I found you parked off the side of the road. You're in my jeep and I'm taking you back to town so Dr. Baker can look at you. You're running a fever and were passed out in your car."

Sara shook her head, "I don't need to see a doctor. I was just resting. I took some of the cough medicine and was waiting for it to start working before I got back on the highway. I didn't want to risk having an accident if I started coughing again."

"Well, I'll feel better after Dr. Baker takes a look. Sara, I ran the plates on the car." Trent paused and watched for her reaction as he made this statement. Instead of guilt or even remorse, he saw immediate fear and panic take over.

Trent had trained at the FBI facility in Quantico for several months prior to returning to his hometown. The bureaucracy of the federal government had been more than he could stomach. He had no doubt in his mind that he would have made a fine profiler and field agent, but Castle Peaks was home, and it suited him just fine.

His training came in useful at times like these, as he evaluated her response to him having checked up on her. Sara was scared, and not because she had stolen her husband's car.

Sara tried to sit up again. She had to convince him to let her go. "The car's not mine. It belongs to my fiancé."

Trent gave her a sideways glance, before saying, "Is your fiancé in the habit of reporting his car stolen when he lets you borrow it?"

David had reported his car stolen. Great! "His car was reported stolen?"

"Yep. And, according to the California Highway Patrol records, someone going by the name of Sara Brownell is the prime suspect. Oh, and she's also wanted for questioning in the attack of David Patterson, the owner of the car."

Sara sank back into the seat. She watched Trent for a minute before asking, "Have you reported in that you found me, yet?"

Trent shook his head, trying to figure out why she was asking. Sara reached out and grabbed his arm, "Please don't. Please don't tell anyone that I'm here. He'll know soon enough because I bought the cough syrup. Please, just take me back to my car and let me go. I didn't steal his car and I can't go back to San Francisco." Sara knew she was begging, but Trent was her only hope. As she finished her plea, another bout of coughing took over and she hugged her ribs, trying to keep the pain from stealing her self-control.

Trent pulled up in front of the medical clinic and turned the jeep off. Turning to look at her, he placed his hand on her back and rubbed slow circles until the coughing fit eased. Talking to himself, he asked, "What are you mixed up in?"

Sara had heard his question, but just shook her head and kept her eyes looking down at her lap. She couldn't go into the details. Who would believe her?

"Let's go see Dr. Baker and then we'll sort the rest of this out."

Thank You

Dear Reader,

Thank you for choosing to read my books out of the thousands that merit reading. I recognize that reading takes time and quietness, so I am grateful that you have designed your lives to allow for this enriching endeavor, whatever the book's title and subject.

Now more than ever before, Amazon reviews and Social Media play vital role in helping individuals make their reading choices. If any of my books have moved you, inspired you, or educated you, please share your reactions with others by posting an Amazon review as well as via email, Facebook, Twitter, Goodreads, -- or even old-fashioned face-to-face conversation! And when you receive my announcement of my new book, please pass it along. Thank you.

For updates about New Releases, as well as exclusive promotions, visit my website and sign up for the VIP mailing list. Click here to get started: www.morrisfenrisbooks.com

I invite you to visit my Facebook page often facebook.com/AuthorMorrisFenris where I post not only my news, but announcements of other authors' work.

For my portfolio of books on Amazon, please visit my Author Page:

Amazon USA:
amazon.com/author/morrisfenris

Amazon UK:
https://www.amazon.co.uk/Morris%20Fenris/e/B00FXLWKRC

You can also contact me by email:
authormorrisfenris@gmail.com

With profound gratitude, and with hope for your continued reading pleasure,

Morris Fenris
Author & Publisher

Made in the USA
Columbia, SC
10 November 2019

82998927R00064